CRUD

on the edge

CANDY

on the edge

DON KERR

COTEAU BOOKS
WWW.COTEAUBOOKS.COM

Cover illustration, Wonderfile/Digital Vision.
Cover and book design by Duncan Campbell.

Printed and bound in Canada at AGMV Marquis.

National Library of Canada Cataloguing in Publication Data

Kerr, Don.
Candy on the edge

ISBN 1-55050-189-5

1. Title.
PS8571.E71C36 2001   JC813'.54   C2001-911228-9
PZ7.K477CA 2001

1 2 3 4 5 6 7 8 9 10

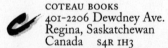

COTEAU BOOKS
401-2206 Dewdney Ave.
Regina, Saskatchewan
Canada   S4R 1H3

AVAILABLE IN THE US FROM
General Distribution Services
4500 Witmer Industrial Estates
Niagara Falls, NY 14305-1386

The publisher gratefully acknowledges the financial assistance of the Saskatchewan Arts Board, the Canada Council for the Arts, the Government of Canada through the Book Publishing Industry Development Program (BPIDP), and the City of Regina Arts Commission, for its publishing program.

To Robyn, Graham, Ryan,
and all the amigos.

chapter 1

"I'M NOT GOING TO TELL YOU TWICE."

She didn't either, thought Candy. She told me three times and that was before I ate breakfast.

"If you go out with her again, if you do, if you go out with her again, I'll tell your dad and then you'll get it missy, then you'll get it."

I kept my eye on my toast. It was a really important piece of toast. Actually it wasn't but I just couldn't look at my mother because I knew as soon as I left the house I was going to see Andrea. Cause I wasn't supposed to.

"If you go out with her again."

That's four, that's four, thought Candy. I'm not going to be a mother, no way. I'll look through the hole between the kitchen and the living room and right out the window. It's like an escape. I can see the elm tree I'm going to walk under and Matichuk's house with the porch and the window where that Gerald, that

1

stupid Gerald, looks out, him and his stupid tongue. I'd rather die than kiss Gerald.

"If you go out with Andrea."

That's five. Andrea is a very bad influence. That's what my mom says. That's what my mom says. She never says anything once. She thinks I'm deaf.

"I'm finished, mom, I'm going to my room."

"And what about Murphy may I ask?"

I knew she'd say that, I knew I'd get to go out.

"I'll walk that dumb dog."

"Do it now."

"Hey, dog, you big dope, c'mon. Wanna go for a walk? Wanna go for a walk?"

The big dope wagged his tail and his backside followed. He whined happily, walked back and forth, put his paws on Candy's shoulder and licked her face.

"Oh yuck, you big dope. C'mon."

"And missy, don't you go see that Andrea. Don't you dare."

That's six. That's six. Do it again, mom, do it again, don't stop now. I'm never going to be a mom, never.

She opened the door into the sun. It was only ten but it was already like a giant oven outside. She blew the hair out of her eyes. Murphy ran in circles on the lawn and then stopped, his tongue hanging out.

"Hey Candy, what you doing?"

"Your nose is running, Gerald."

He rubbed it.

"You dipstick, Gerald."

"You dope bucket."

"You barney."

"Oh no, not that, not that."

"Bye Gerald, your mommy wants you."

And Candy was around the corner, calling to Murphy to keep up and Murphy the dog thought, she's my favourite person in the world right now. She cut down the alley behind Gerald's house, over to nineteenth and kept on going, Murphy trotting behind her, and there was Andrea's house. It was a bungalow her mother sniffed at. It didn't have any paint. Well, it did have paint, but that was a long time ago, hell's bells said her dad, it hasn't been painted since Noah's Ark.

Candy told Murphy to sit down and knocked at the door. Murphy knocked too, with his tail. He liked it at Patenaudes'. Mrs. P. always gave him scraps and scratched his ears.

"C'mon in, whoever you are. Door ain't locked."

It was only a screen door anyway and Candy went in. The front room was always a mess, with newspapers on one chair and food left on the coffee table which had one leg bandaged and Candy had said like it had been to the table hospital and there was a towel on the TV and her mom who was very neat would have had a flaming fit but it didn't bother Candy who was used to it. Her dad said her mom never had a hair out of place except in a high wind.

"Hi Candy. Nice to see ya and Murphy. Hi Murph."

"Hi Mrs. Patenaude, is Andrea in?"

"Andrea!!!" Mrs. Patenaude was a great shouter. "She was out in the yard, go have a look. Hey Murph, I got a piece of pie for you."

The kitchen was kind of rough too, with linoleum worn and broken in one corner. Candy liked the cupboards curving at the edges and the built-in flour bin and they even had a pantry only everything just sat on shelves. There was a red arborite counter – that's what Mrs. P. called it when she ran her hand over it cause it was cool. But it had cuts in it and you could see the pipes under the sink that had two taps not just one. Candy went outside.

"Andrea!! Here's a brush, Candy. Murphy needs a good brush."

The backyard lawn had every kind of green thing in it and Mrs. P. mowed it down once a month, "whether it needs it or not." It needed it again. Candy sat on the top of the stoop, cause she knew the grass was full of mosquitoes but they must be tired too in the heat. She brushed the dog who kept his ears back and sat very still.

"Wonder where Andrea is Murphy? You like that pie? You like a nice brush? Gotta be home soon or Mom will start wondering. Don't tell on me dog, say we went to the river, okay? That's a good dog."

The good dog wagged his tail. Dog was one of his favourite words. "You like my Lion King wristwatch?" Murphy did and licked Candy's arm. What a nice dog.

Candy stood on the top of the stoop but couldn't see Andrea. Why do people have such high fences? Andrea said they put them up to keep her out. Their own fence was way higher than she was, "to keep out the prying eyes," her mom said, maybe so they wouldn't know what her dad was barbecuing. They had a fancy gas barbecue. Her dad was an expert on it. He said so himself. Candy helped by bringing out the condiments and setting the wooden table.

"No Andrea?"

"Nope. I gotta get home. Tell Andrea I was here."

"Want her to phone?"

"No, better not."

"Never know where that girl's got to."

Candy walked the long way home so her mom wouldn't know where she'd been. She took the dog through the back gate. She had to stand tiptoe to undo the stupid latch. She lay in the grass. Her dad cut the grass every Sunday. She was sweating now but she didn't care. She stayed right in the sun and looked up at the sky, watching clouds, wispy ones, like her grampa's hair, then big fat ones coming from over Oleniuks' house. There was a whale but it got snagged on the maple tree and became an island in the blue sea. How far does blue go? A lot of kilometres. She could hear the buzzing of a small plane and put her hand over her eyes to keep the sun out and watched the plane like a giant insect, like a dragonfly, buzz past the sun, under the biggest cloud in the sky and across her backyard and disappear towards Andrea's. I bet he can't even see me. I'm just a speck. Murphy faloomped himself right beside her.

"Move over, you dang dog."

"Is that you, Candy?"

Oh no, captured again.

"Is that you, Candy?"

chapter 2

"LOOK AFTER NORMAN, CANDY, I HAVE TO GET groceries, be back in an hour, missy."

"Okay mom. Hey Norman, what you doin baby?"

Norman was eighteen months old, could walk and run with one foot way to the left and one foot way to the right. "Isn't that funny?" said her mom. "Mom, how'd you think you'd walk if you were wearing diapers?" Candy thought Norman was the funniest thing she'd ever seen. He was in the living room trying to turn Murphy into a giant pillow. Murphy got bugged and moved away and Norman ran after him and hugged him. Murphy looked at Candy. Take this kid off me, he said, and she grabbed Norman and threw him in the air and caught him. He laughed so hard she had to do it again, and again.

"Once more?"

He put his hands up and said, "Canny, Canny."

Up he went. He had some real words like
mine, yes, no, and Canny and Murray the dog
and spireman – that was Spiderman – and dirats
– that was dirty rats Candy was teaching him to
say when he was mad. Candy thought her own
name was stupid because people made fun of it
like Candy is handy and dandy and other stupid
stuff but Norman, who would call a kid
Norman? A poor little baby who couldn't
defend himself. That was her grampa's name but
it was okay in a grampa. She called him Carboy
because he walked around with a toy car in each
hand. He wouldn't play with Candy's old Barbie
stuff. That's cause he was a boy. She rolled
Carboy on his back and tickled him till he
squirmed off the couch and ran away.

"Here I come, Carboy."

He shrieked and Candy stalked him. She
could never tell which way he'd go. He was like
a video game, bouncing all over the place.

"Hey, Carboy, want to play ball?"

She sat him at the table and rolled a small
cloth ball at him. He grabbed it and said,
"hoyyeahwah," and rolled it back.

"Hey, good one, Carboy, good one."

He clapped his hands for himself and he
rolled it back, his eyes intent on the ball.

"Hoyyeahwah."

"Roll it to me, okay? Here it comes back to you."

"Hoyyeahwah."

"C'mon, Carboy, throw it back. You hiding it, you little tricker?"

Candy crawled under the table. Carboy shrieked "hoyyeahwah" when she popped up and got the ball where he'd hidden it behind his back, and she went back and rolled it again and Carboy hid it again and looked innocent as a baby.

"You little tricker. I'm gonna tell mom and dad what a little tricker you are."

The phone rang once only. That's Andrea's signal to phone back. Candy hung Carboy on her hip, walked into the kitchen and phoned Andrea.

"Hello, Candyass. Are you free?"

"My mom's out."

"C'mon over."

"Can't. I'm looking after superkid. Hey, you know what he did? We were playing ball on the table and he started hiding it behind his back. Pretty smart eh?"

"That's really interesting, Candyass."

"Yeah, well it was."

"I got some guys for you to meet."

"Yeah?"

"Yeah. We're meetin at the school after supper, like maybe eight. Be there if you dare."

"Hey, Andrea. Where were you this morning when I came over?"

"Doin my homework, you know me."

"Oh yeah, who with?"

"Eight o'clock."

"So whatcha doin?"

"I'm talkin to you, Candycane."

"What's their names?"

"I can't give that info on the telephone. It might be bugged by your mom."

"Or your mom."

"My mom? She can't even find the phone."

"So what're you doin?"

"I'm hangin up."

Candy stuck her baby brother in front of the TV and put the "Wallace and Grommit" video on and he climbed on the couch and watched and grinned. He watched it every day. Candy forgot Andrea and her message and laughed at Carboy with cars in each hand and a dumb grin on his face. Murphy jumped on the couch that was forbidden territory, watched Candy to see if it was okay. She scratched his ears so he rolled on his back and said pet me, love me, and she scratched his belly.

"Hey Candy, Candy, help me unload the car."

Oh, oh, the warlord's here. "Down Murphy, down," and the dog went to its place by the door so he could always see both ways and was innocent as a dog. Carboy went running for his mom.

"Mom, mom, mom."

She picked him up and nuzzled him.

"Were there any phone calls?"

"None for you mom."

Candy went to the car and brought in plastic bags of groceries, helped her mom put them in the fridge and wondered how she could get out of the house tonight.

chapter 3

CANDY PHONED KATH TO ASK A FAVOUR, TO tell her mom if she phoned that she and Kath were studying. Kath said she didn't want to lie. Candy promised her a Céline Dion CD if her mom phoned.

"Cause maybe she won't. She doesn't follow me all the time."

"She'll get you a cellphone like Marcie's mom to keep track of you."

"Gross, eh? You'll do it, won't you? Be best friends, Kath. C'mon, Kath. You're not goin out, are you?"

"No."

"Okay – deal? Best friends."

"I don't know. Alright. Okay."

"Thanks, you're a princess."

Candy hung up and did a high-five with herself and decided what to wear. Her hair was done. Her mom had made braids and she looked like Pippi stupid Longstocking. It was too cute so she put on her oldest jeans to look tough and the black short-sleeve blouse her mom hated. Her mom always dressed so she looked like a rainbow. Her mom was not cool. She was always in stuff like aquamarine and chartreuse and flamingo pink. Sometimes she looked like the inside of a cantaloupe. Candy hated walking with her mom at parents' night even if her mom worked out at Fitness Belles and didn't look old like her father but he just wore whatever and looked okay and laughed at her when she wanted a rose tattoo on her arm, not like her mom who had another flaming fit.

At 7:30 Candy told her mom she was going to do homework and went out and there was Gerald sitting on the front steps pretending to read.

"Hey, bandy Candy, I got a new video game."

"Your nose is running, Gerald."

"So's your big mouth."

"You turkey leg."

"Dirt bag."

"Booger brain."

"Hogwash."

"Pig head."

She'd made up insults in advance.

"Space girl."

"Brain soup."

"Bosom buddies."

"Dork head."

"Hey, wait."

Gerald went into his house and came back out wearing a toque.

"So what's that?"

"Safe thinking."

Candy laughed. "You win this time, chicken gizzard."

"See you, Candy, pretty, pretty, pretty Candy."

He sounded like he was calling a cat. Candy walked towards Kath's and did her usual switcheroo and headed for school. Seemed weird wanting to go to school. It was June, two weeks left and Mr. Lestock was grumpy. It was an old school with towers like a medieval castle but inside it was new. Grade Eights had control. They were the kings. They walked like they knew everything, like about sex and smoking and bands and talked in groups about stuff nobody else knew like filter tips or tattoos on Ramon the dream guy and where and who's done it and what kinda car they wanted to drive with a guy in. There were drippy Grade Eights who worked all the time at school and answered questions for Loopy Lestock without even being asked. Candy got good marks so she was outside the tough gang. Kath was out of it and wanted in to Candy's nice group. Gerald was just out of it, a wimp, like he got really good marks and he didn't care what he looked like and didn't play sports, not even hockey, and he was so dumb at gym he had to climb up on the parallel bars with a chair, loser, loser, loser, and he didn't even know it. Candy had her own girl-friends since Grade One but they were kind of boring now and she wanted in the cool gang, the one Andrea was in, cause they were myste-rious.

When Candy got to school no one was there. She walked around the building, feeling stupid. She never knew what Andrea would do. Would she even come? She waited. She wished she smoked. She'd have something to do. At least it wasn't as hot out now but she was still sweating from the walk. Should have worn shorts. She shook the neck of her blouse and blew down it. Maybe if I don't move, if I don't move an inch, I'll cool off. I'll concentrate. I'll tell my body, cool off. I'll start with my arms. Hey there's Andrea. She's wearing jeans too, and a bright pink halter. Yuck.

"Hey, Andrea."

"Hey, Candy."

Andrea had her cigarettes in her backpack and lit one, a Rothmans out of a red package.

"Want a smoke?"

"No thank you."

Smoking looked great. Andrea held it between her forefinger and second finger, like a bird. It was cool. She inhaled like it was nothing, like she did it all the time. If you smoked you didn't have to talk. Candy was scared to take a smoke.

"So, who are your friends?"

"You'll see, you just gotta wait."

She blew smoke out. If I smoked, Candy thought, my mom would kill me. She'd smell it. She'd kill me dead on the spot. They said in school, the health officer, that such awful things could happen to you if you smoked. They haven't met my mom. She'd be worse. Dad used to smoke. Why'd he quit?

"Does your mom care if you smoke?"

"She buys em for me, dopey. She wants company."

I should smoke. If she offers again I'll take one.

"What're we sposed to read for Monday, Candy?"

"It's some poems."

"Poems? Torture, torture, torture."

"By Longfellow."

"Longfellow. I'd like to meet him."

"He's dead."

"No kidden? You know everything, don't you, drip."

Andrea got up and walked to the corner. She's got real breasts, thought Candy, not little ones. She's sure lucky. I need a cigarette. If I had a cigarette I'd be like Andrea.

"Hey Candyass, c'mere. They're comin."

Two girls who wore jeans and black blouses walked real slow across the street, so the car had to stop for them. One of them was really big. Candy was nervous. And excited. Andrea yelled.

"Hey, you guys, over here."

chapter 4

THE FOUR GIRLS SAT AT A BOOTH IN THE RED Robin Café, Candy with her Diet Coke, Rhonda with her Coke and chips, Andrea with chips and gravy, Sam with black coffee. Rhonda poured ketchup over the chips.

"You're gonna drown in ketchup," said Sam.

"Are there fries under there?" asked Candy.

Rhonda looked at her.

"I like ketchup."

"She puts it on her apple pie."

"Blow it out your other ear, Candy," said Andrea.

"Ketchup loves potatoes," said Candy.

"Huh."

"That's one of the songs my dad sings."

Candy was surprised at herself. She was talking. She thought she'd be tongue-tied. Sam scared her. She liked her, but she was scared of her too. Sam was taller and way bigger, like fat but big too, with a dagger tattoo on her right arm and some kind of bird on the other arm. Rhonda had scary eyes.

"What's that bird?" asked Candy.

"It's a crow, you dipstick, you Candyass," said Andrea.

"Candy, my name is Candy."

"Candy, okay. I'm Sam, so shake on it."

"Samantha," said Rhonda who said mostly nothing.

Sam looked hard at her. Sam was bigger than any of the boys she knew. Rhonda went back to her chips and ate them so fast you could hardly see them go.

"She always eats like that. She's feedin a worm, aintcha, Rhon? Feedin a worm."

"Hey, if she's Ron and you're Sam, then I'm Ann and you're Can. Hey Can, hey garbage can."

"Least that owly bugger ain't in here tonight," said Sam.

"Who?"

"The guy that runs the place, yknow, threw us out, right Rhon?"

"Mr. Wilhelm?"

"That's the one. So las week we're in here and we're mad, yknow, well I'm mad so we start sayin" – Sam looked around, saw a waitress watching them – "well, anyways you know we used the f word and stuff. I mean I was mad."

"Why?" asked Candy.

"Keep your nose on your own face where it belongs. Anyway that four-eyed owl tells us to clean up our language or he'll throw us out so I said" – she looked around again – "well, you know what I said so he booted us out. That waitress must be his henchman."

"It's on accounta her stepdad," said Rhonda. "She was so mad she punched him out."

Rhonda was on her second plate of chips and ketchup.

"You need a shovel, Rhonda," said Candy.

Rhonda looked at Candy so hard it felt like daggers going through her. Rhonda stood up, her fork in her hand, but Sam grabbed her and sat her down hard, gave her a cigarette and had one herself.

"He deserved it, my stepdad. He's always after me. He deserved it. Cool it, Rhon."

"What about your mom?" asked Candy, keeping an eye on Rhonda who was watching her all the time.

"Well, I told her once and she belted me. Who's got a decent mom, eh Rhon?"

"Or dad," said Andrea.

"My mom's sure tough," said Candy.

"She beat you?"

"No, but she's always on my case, she always keeps tabs, like if she knew I was here I'd be in for it, boy, I'd be really in for it."

"She's got a tough life," said Andrea.

"I got a girlfriend Marcie," said Candy. "Her mom bought her a cellphone so she'd always know where she was. Isn't that awful?"

"That's terrible," said Andrea in a tone that said what a drip you are, Candy.

"I'd like a cellphone, hey, Rhon? Rhonda."

"Sure."

"So Candy, where would you get a cellphone?"

"Well, SaskTel stores, or Radio Shack."

"Want a smoke?"

"No thank you."

Sam, Andrea and Rhonda smoked like old pros. Candy paid attention to the bottom of her Coke.

"Whatcha doin after school tomorrow?"

"Nothin," said Candy.

"Wanna go downtown with us?"

"Sure, sure."

"Okay, meetcha here at four and we'll walk down. Do some shoppin at the Plaza, right Andrea? Okay Rhonda?"

Rhonda nodded, looking at her chips again. Candy walked home excited. This is everything her home wasn't, her completely neat home, with her completely neat room, and her completely neat yard. Thank goodness for that dumb dog and that crazy Carboy, the number one mess-maker in the world. If there was something to dump he'd dump it. That gave her mom something to do, cleaning up after Carboy. Wonder why Rhonda doesn't talk? Would she have stuck a fork in me? She sure looked mad. Sam liked me, I could tell. I like her better than Andrea. My dad's nice to me, not like that awful stepdad. Candy walked in the front door. Her mom and dad were watching TV and didn't see her. My girlfriends'll die to see me with Sam. She went up to her room, kicked off her shoes and took off her jeans that were so hot and went to lie down on the bed but she couldn't sleep. She was jumpy. She was just plain excited. She went out in the backyard and wrestled with Murphy.

chapter 5

CANDY AND SAM MET OUTSIDE THE RED ROBIN and walked across the bridge downtown. Candy knew they'd be seen together, by Gerald and Kath and everyone else in school. Let them eat their hearts out, me walking with Sam. Yeah, yeah, yeah.

"Candy, you're lookin real pretty."

"Gee thanks. I gotta be neat at school.'

Candy had on a white skirt and a pale blue blouse. Sam wore a brown skirt and a jean jacket so she didn't look as tough as when she met her at school.

"Can I ask, can I ask, how come you got tattoos?"

"You like em?"

"I guess. I dunno."

"Look."

"Holy cow."

Sam had lifted her jacket to show a ring on her navel.

"Did it hurt?"

"My mom hated it so I did it. Know what I mean?"

"Yes I do, I sure do."

"You done anything to your mom?"

"No."

There was a light breeze so it was both hot and cool and the river was hundreds of small waves. The sun made all the buildings look nice and Candy was happy.

"You livin at home?"

"Yes."

"I ain't."

"Cause of your stepdad?"

"Keep your nose on your face."

"Sorry. Why'd you get the tattoos? I mean, was that like to get back at your mom?"

"I went out with this guy. He was older. He wasn't too bright but I did him a deal. If he quit doin B and Es I'd get a tattoo with him."

"Holy smokes."

"He's a jerk. He's in detention in Kilburn."

Candy thought, holy smoke. She wanted to keep talking. She wanted to know who Sam was. She was like a story she was reading. How'd Andrea get to know her? Why's she want to be my friend? Guess I'm lucky.

"Are you in school, Sam?"

"Spose to be. Remedial Grade Nine. That's cause I'm dumb."

Candy thought, she isn't dumb. Maybe she can't read. Candy read a book a week and her mom thought that was great. She read books about dogs and animals maybe because she liked Babar stories and Curious George so much when she was little.

"You're dumb like a fox," Candy said.

Sam looked at her, patted her lightly on her back with her big paw.

"We're gonna meet Rhon and Andy at the Plaza. You need a clock radio?"

"No, not really."

"Well today you're goin in Radio Shack and you're gonna ask the guy you wanta see clock radios. Okay?"

"I guess."

"You're doin it for me, Candy. I'll owe you one."

"Okay. Sure."

Candy thought, I guess it's okay, I guess. At the Plaza they found Andrea and Rhonda browsing in the clothes at Sears. Rhonda was very serious holding a short-sleeved sweater against herself. Andrea was nodding that's a good one. She was wearing her best stuff. She'd skipped school again.

"Hey guys."

"Hi Sam, hi Candy."

Rhonda just put the sweater down and walked towards Radio Shack.

"Hey," said Sam, "a plan. I'll leave by Sears, Rhon, you go down the Plaza."

"Okay."

"Andy you can, uh, wait for us here. Keep your eyes open. Okay Candy, let's go shoppin, like ask that guy about seein clock radios. You don't got to buy it, just talk, okay?"

Candy walked to the counter and asked what kind of clock radios they had and what prices and he said, "What would you like to spend?"

"I'm not going to buy one but my dad's going to buy me a birthday present so I thought I'd help him out."

"Here's one at $49.99 with good FM."

"What about that one?"

"Oh that's over a hundred but you can play tapes on it too."

"Neat. Would you write its number and price on a piece of paper for me?"

He did it and Candy said, "Thanks a lot for all of your help," sounding just like her mom. When she walked out Sam was nowhere to be seen, or Andrea. She saw Rhonda on the other side of the mall. Candy didn't say anything because she was afraid to talk to Rhonda. As Rhonda walked past a shop she picked a vest off a hanger and put it in her Sears bag. She stole it, thought Candy, she stole it! Candy followed and saw Rhonda drop a black T-shirt into the bag and then take the elevator down and leave the Plaza. Jeez, thought Candy, I'd never do that. It's awful, it's stealing. It sure looked easy.

chapter 6

DOUG AND TRICIA WERE SITTING IN THE LIVING room, he in his reclining chair with the stool attached, so when he leaned back it came out, she on the flowered couch with her feet curled under her bum. Candy had gone to bed an hour ago. They'd just finished the CBC news. Tricia spoke. She didn't want to have an argument with her husband but it had to be said.

"I have to tell you Candy's hanging out with new friends and they're not nice girls."

"Andrea again."

"Well yes, but much worse now, the Didick girl, what's her name? Samantha. Her father's Larry, you know the one."

"Who ran off with the Narfason's car and has never been seen since."

"Her mother's in jail for shoplifting and I'm scared. Crystal. That's her name."

"Have you met her?"

"Crystal?"

"No, no, Samantha."

"I haven't but she's been in lots of trouble."

"Maybe she's okay."

"That's just like you, pretend everyone's nice and nothing's wrong. Candy's going out with the worst girls. And the other one, Rhonda, who can't rub two sticks together. I mean they're remedial and they're older, they're in high school, and they're into break and enters, did you know that?"

"I'm going for a beer."

Doug walked into the kitchen, twisted a cap off a lite and wished Tricia would button her lip. He hated arguments. He hated them. He never won. He knew the onslaught would continue. He knew it. He knew it in his bones. He went back to his chair and picked up the paper he'd already read.

"What are you going to do about it?"

"Candy's great. She'll be okay."

"You're impossible. Your daughter is now friends with the worst girls and they're thieves and they take stuff."

"How do you know?"

"I talked with Mrs. Kutz, I met her at the Co-op, the social worker who visits the school, and she knew Candy was out with them."

"Candy knows we love her. She'll be okay."

"So I have to be the heavy again. I always

have to be the heavy. You think if you smile and
say hi Candy and love her, everything'll be okay.
You're always the nice one. It's just not fair."

I knew it, he thought. I knew it. I'd get
caught, I'd lose, I'll have to do something. I hate
that.

Tricia thought, I can't take it anymore. I can't
always yell at her. Why can't I shut up? Why do
I always nag? No. I'm in the right. Those girls
are scary. Andrea too. Her mother lets her do
whatever she wants. Candy might take drugs or
become a thief, or die in a car crash with some
drunk driver. He has to see how tough it is. It's
not fair to leave it to me!

"What do you want me to do?"

"Just talk to her."

"Tell me about these girls. I don't know what
to say."

"Ask her."

"I'm sure everything will be okay."

"Douglas, for goodness sakes, wake up. Sure
she's okay, she's great with the infant prodigy,
she does great in school, she's pretty as a button,
but what about her new friends, like why does
she even need such friends? I don't understand
her, and what if they make her do things like
steal or take drugs, I mean why does Candy
want such friends? I'm scared."

Doug stood up and reached for Tricia's hand
and pulled her up and hugged her. She felt at

home, she felt like she was twenty again and saw Doug the basketball player who was so easygoing and funny. Help me, she said to herself, help me. Doug thought she still feels good, she's still a real handful, a bit bigger since the kids but nice, real nice. Caught, caught again.

Candy had heard her parents talking about her and had slipped out of her bedroom to the top of the stairs to listen. She scurried quickly to bed, pretended to be asleep and in two minutes she was.

chapter 7

"HELLO SAM, IT'S CANDY."

"Hi Candy. How'd you get this number?"

"Andrea had it in her book. I peeked."

"Yeah."

"So I wanta tell you about cellphones."

"Yeah."

"Cause like, they won't work unless you sign up to a company."

"Yeah."

"And, uh, like, the companies know the number of each phone."

"So."

"So like, if someone steals one they shouldn't sign up to use them. Or they'll be caught."

"How do you know all this?"

"I asked my dad. He knows."

"Why are you telling me, Candy?"

"Well, like, if anybody stole a cellphone they should throw it in the garbage cause if anyone tries to use it they'll know it was stolen."

"Why'd you ask your dad?"

"I saw Rhonda shoplifting at the Plaza and you split awful fast."

"You tell anyone?"

"Course not. And I just asked my dad in general like."

"Well, thanks for the call, Candy."

"Kay, Sam, bye."

Sam went into her stash at the back of the closet, pulled the cellphone out from under a sweater, put it into a plastic bag in the kitchen, walked out the side door of the basement flat, looked around, walked down the alley and dumped the useless thing in somebody else's giant green garbage bin and kept going to Broadway to meet Ramon who had a case of beer and they went back to her place because he still had parents. Ramon was the coolest guy Sam knew. He was in Grade Eleven and he'd been in Kilburn twice, once for B and E, and once for having burglary tools on him. He liked Sam cause she knew everything and was bigger than him and could protect him and liked him a lot.

"Hey Ramon, you know you can't steal cell-phones."

"Get out of here. You can steal anything you want."

"But they got numbers and if you use them you get caught."

"That's a bad trip. How you know that, Samantha?"

She loved her name out full when Ramon said it.

"How you know that?"

"I learned. So you gotta throw it out, sorry, it'll land you back."

"Shit."

"You use it?"

"I signed up, I signed up, did not use my own name, I never do that with hot stuff."

"Where is it?"

Ramon pulled it out of his jean jacket pocket.

"I got to dump it, right?"

"You got to dump it."

CANDY TOOK THE DANG DOG MURPHY FOR A walk. She had to go think things over. Rhonda scared her. She stole. She didn't know what was going on inside her. Who knew what she'd do next? It was another great day and the dog jumped up and grabbed the lead in his mouth and threw it back and forth like an enemy. Candy laughed.

"What a dopey dog. Hey."

She stretched her arm as high as her head and the dang dog jumped for it. She shook the lead and Murphy went crazy.

"Dopey dog."

Oh no, Gerald again, I'm going to have to start leaving by the back door, Candy thought.

"Hey nas goof," said Gerald.

"Rattlebrain."

"Dartlestuff."

"Goosesniffer."

"Snaggle fart."

"Gerald, haven't you anything better to do?"

"Ratsnort."

"Cowsniff."

"Hey, Candy, yknow, if you need my help, like, in any way, I'd help."

"Doodlebug."

"Skunkpelt."

"Rabbit tail and everything under it. And I'm outa here, Gerald lame brain."

"See you, panda candy."

Candy was worn out. She thought, my brain's sore. I can't keep it up with Gerald. I'm tired of having to write out insults to him. Does he just make them up on the spot? She walked to the river. Murphy liked that walk and sniffed madly. Ugh, dogs, thought Candy. I wouldn't want to be that close to the earth, sniffing dog pee and stuff. Candy sat on a bench and told Murphy to sit. He did. He liked Candy telling him to do things so he could prove how good a dog he was and they should keep him forever. He put his head on his paws and looked sad as he could. That always gets them, he thought.

Candy looked at the city over the river, the downtown. She breathed out and tried to relax. She had this trick – she learned it in an exercise class – of breathing hard then soft until her body went quiet and her breathing was real slow. There were clouds on the horizon, coming in from the west, wispy clouds. There was a breeze that cooled her off after the walk. There was something dark at the back of her mind. She tried to look at it. Was it Andrea? Do I want to see Andrea? Do I like Samantha better? My new best friend. Does she steal? I feel so small beside her. Should I have phoned her like I did? I was trying to help. In case she stole a cellphone. My dad wants to see me after supper. Do they know? I liked it at the Plaza. I was good, I know that guy believed me. Rhonda scares me, scares me silly. I don't like her. I don't like her. I wanta see Sam again. She must steal too. I'll try to be nice to Andrea even if she does make fun of me. Why'd she want me to meet Sam and Rhonda? Hey dang dog, gimme a kiss. Oh, your nose is wet. Yuck.

chapter 8

HER DAD TOOK CANDY FOR LUNCH AT Fuddruckers. She knew he was going to talk about Sam and Rhonda, only they talked about nothing, well, some important stuff like about Norman and how funny he was stuffing toys down his sleepers and clunking when he walked. Candy laughed about how she emptied him and he started all over, very serious like it was his job, said her dad. "Candy M" said the loudspeaker and they got their hamburgers and loaded them up, only Candy drew the line at sauerkraut like her dad put on. She got her Coke, he got his coffee. Candy talked about Murphy who knocked over Carboy once, I mean Norman, with his big tail and Norman laughed and laughed.

"How's school?"

"I'm doing good. I got an A on my composition, you know the one I interviewed you for."

"Oh yeah, right. Didn't know you'd finished."

"We got new computers at school, from the government, they gave new computers, so I did it there. They're really neat. Oh there's blood coming out of your burger!"

"Listen close, can you hear that cow moo? So how are your friends?"

"You mean Andrea, don't you?"

"How's she do in school?"

"She's smart, you know, but she doesn't care. I'm smarter than she is but she'd be okay if she tried. I used to help her with homework but she doesn't work and she skips and she's in trouble with Mr. Lestock. She's in his bad books, like she might not get her Grade Eight but I like her and her mom and when Murphy and I visit her mom is great and Murphy barks and jumps when we get to the yard cause he'll get a treat and Mrs. Patenaude is really nice to me'n I wish I could invite Andrea back home. Maybe not, maybe she's just too far gone but I don't think mom's fair."

Candy couldn't stop talking. She'd never said anything about Andrea to her dad before. He never asked anything. Candy ate her hamburger, dipped her chips in ketchup and cheese sauce. Her dad tried one that way. "Hey, that's pretty good." He had vinegar all over his chips and the sauerkraut leaked out of the hamburger over them. Candy tried one of his. "Oh yuck." Her dad laughed.

"That's too bad about Andrea. She'll have a tough time without school."

"Yeah."

"You know your mom and I want you to go to university."

"I know."

There was a silence. More chips. Three kids ran by to play the jukebox. More names were called. Stephanie D. Billy K. Her dad went and refilled his coffee. Candy waited. Will he ask about Sam and Rhonda? She drank her Coke.

"So, we're going to take a trip to Vancouver soon as school's over. I got my holidays set."

"Through the mountains?"

"Can't get to Vancouver without going through mountains. You'll have to help out with Norman – with Carboy – give your mom a break."

"Sure, sure, dad."

"We need to find a place for Murphy for three weeks."

"Can't we take him?"

"Some places don't want dogs, especially big dogs."

"I'd look after him."

"Mom says no but we'll find a good kennel. Think of him as going to school with other dogs. Learn a trade like rounding up girls who skip school. Anyway, nice to talk with you, Candy, but I gotta get back to work, make enough money to go on a trip."

"I'm gonna go to university, yknow."

Candy hugged her dad. He never said a thing about Sam and Rhonda. Now I'll bet he's in trouble with mom.

ANDREA WAS AT SCHOOL ON MONDAY. MR. Lestock welcomed her in his usual way. "Miss Patenaude, how nice of you to grace us with your presence." At recess Andrea told Candy Sam wanted her to phone. Candy had put off talking to Sam all weekend. She wanted to. She really wanted to, but she was nervous about stealing so she didn't phone but after school Candy was excited. Her mom was in the backyard watering her garden. Candy thought, I can talk to Sam again. She dialed. She watched her finger as it touched each number. She heard the ring, three, four. I should hang up she thought in a panic, bit her nail. There was no answer and she put the phone back with relief. She went out back and asked her mom if she could help and weeded between the carrot rows. Her mom was surprised.

"Want to take Murphy for a walk?"

"Sure. Come on dumb dog, we'll go to the river. Okay?"

And off they went, only Candy's feet took her to the river the long way, down the alley where Sam had her basement apartment. Candy's heart was beating as she went past.

"Hey Candy."

She turned and there was Sam yelling out the window.

"Wait a sec."

"Sit down, Murphy."

Sam came out in jeans and a black T-shirt. Ramon came out too. Candy's heart jumped. Cause he was the coolest guy around. Everyone knew that. Her girlfriends drooled over him. He was in a T-shirt so his tattoos shone in the sun. His skin was kinda dark. And he had this killer grin.

"Whatcha doin, Candy?"

"Just walking Murphy."

"Nice dog you got," said Ramon, squatting before him and rubbing his nose.

"You met Ramon, Candy?"

"No. Hi."

She didn't know she could still talk cause her heart was beating or something inside was mixed up.

"Hey hi, Candy."

He still had a big grin.

"Sam said you was pretty."

Candy was tongue-tied now. This was the guy all her girlfriends talked about, all the time. Where was he from? Like Chile or someplace down there.

"Gotta walk Murphy."

She couldn't say anything else. That was a safe thing to say.

"Okay," said Ramon. "You drop in tomorrow, okay, see you then, Candy."

"Bye."

When she heard Ramon say Candy it was like hearing her own name for the first time, and she walked down the alley with her back on fire because his eyes were on her.

chapter 9

CANDY COULDN'T PAY ATTENTION IN SCHOOL. "Candy McFarlane, Miss McFarlane, are you with us today?" That was Mr. Lestock. "I know school is a punishment for children but you've only a week till freedom. Until then you'll pay attention to your education."

Candy couldn't get her mind away from Ramon. She could see him after school. When she thought of that her mind went all over the place. She couldn't control her dream. She didn't care what her mom thought. Ramon was so so cool, so sexy. Her mom had done her Pippi Longstocking hair because she thought it was cute like she was still eight years old. But after school she'd take the elastic band off and let her hair fall down her back. She was a brunette. She'd read that in one of her mom's women's magazines. A brunette. She loved the sound of the word and she loved her hair, which was thick. She hated her freckles. How could a serious girl have freckles? They were demeaning. "Miss McFarlane, Miss McFarlane, does British Columbia have a capital?" Victoria. "Thank you. And Washington State. That's in America." Olympia. "Ah, that's very good and named after what mountain?" Olympus. "Thank you, Candy, you may go back to sleep again." It was a review. They'd answered those questions before. "Ah, the window. You're looking out the window. And it is dirty. Need to clean that window for you, Candy. Now Gerald, Washington is in D.C., and what does the D.C. stand for?" Somebody said under their breath AC/DC and Mr. Lestock thanked whoever it was and Gerald said District of Columbia. "And who is that named after?" and Gerald said, "Christopher Columbus who discovered the new world" and Angela Badger said, "People were here already" and Mr. Lestock said, "They were indeed and Columbus thought he was in India and didn't know which way was up." Candy heard it all from a long way away and then the bell rang.

"Hey, Candy Kane. Where you goin so fast?"

"How come you're in school again, Andrea?"

"My mom said if I don't go I get no smokes. Where you goin so fast?"

"None a your business."

"I'm goin with you."

"I'm just going home."

"I'll walk you home. Ain't hardly seen you since the Plaza. You never phone or nothin. You seen Sam?"

"You know my mom."

Now Candy couldn't see Ramon. She had to walk home. She couldn't take her stupid hair down. She wanted Andrea to buzz off.

"You got your dumb hair on again. Everybody laughs at you, yknow."

"Hey, girl people."

It was Gerald who'd caught up with them.

"Oh not you," said Andrea, "go drip on someone else."

Now she was trapped by both of them. She'd have to go home. There was no way out. She was captured.

"Gerald, go get lost."

"Ah Andrea, ants-in-her-pants."

"You jerk."

"Thick head."

"What a dope."

"Tits for brains."

"Just leave us alone," yelled Andrea.

"Dead head."

"You can't win, Andrea," said Candy. "I know."

"What a stupid little boy."

"Smart tart."

"Darn you."

"Fart finger."

When they reached her house, Candy said bye and went inside. Gerald said fart finger again to Andrea, and went into his house. Andrea, mad as could be, started to walk home and thought, no way, I'm gonna see Sam. I'll show them.

There was a note on the kitchen table to Candy from her mom. "Sorry, Candy. I had to go to the neighbourhood meeting. Have a cookie, back at six," and Candy jumped in the air, Murphy barked and jumped with her. "I gotta go, Murph," only he did tail wag, tail wag.

"Okay, okay, short walk, okay?"

Absolutely, said Murphy. Short walk, with my best friend, and take your plastic bag because I'm ready to go.

Candy took a plastic bag and they set off but when Candy came to the corner where she'd turn and take Murphy back home she kept going, towards the river, to Sam's. She did her bag trick by a bush cause Murphy was a couth dog. When she turned down the alley toward Sam's she saw Andrea talking to Ramon and stepped quickly back so she wouldn't be seen and wanted to cry, but somebody would see her so she walked past the nice houses her mom liked, the ones from before the war, she said. But Candy couldn't see anything. There was a film of tears in her eyes. Murphy began to jump at his leash and shake it in his mouth like a rat.

Candy didn't react so he just walked home like a serious dog. She left him in the backyard and walked up to her room like a sleep-walker and cried and cried. She knew she was being stupid. Why would Ramon look at her? It didn't matter. She cried and cried. He's probably Sam's guy anyway. It didn't matter, she still cried.

chapter 10

CANDY WAS SAD AND MAD AND COULDN'T sleep. She was so mad at that busybody Andrea. Serve her right to fail. She's my enemy. I don't care what happens to her. I wish I knew curses. I'd give her acne. I'd make her hair fall out. I'd make her breasts shrink. I'll never see Ramon again. He said I'm cute. She planned punishment after punishment for Andrea. She fell asleep. She didn't want to. She'd decided to stay awake forever to hate Andrea. After she'd punched her out and made her wear Pippi Longstocking hair and flamingo shorts and a green blouse, she fell asleep. She was never going to fall asleep again. She thought of Ramon going away and was sad and fell asleep. She was going to stay awake forever dreaming of Ramon. No! It was stupid. Andrea knew how to get guys. I don't. I'm useless. So what if I'm good at school. So what. If you're unhappy for life who cares.

She fell asleep. I'm never going to fall asleep. I got so much to think about. She fell asleep.

Next morning Candy told her mom she'd never wear those dumb pigtails again. "Everybody's laughing at me. So leave me alone. I can brush my own hair, okay, lemme alone." Tricia walked out of the bedroom. Candy didn't need her anymore. Tricia didn't turn on the TV. She couldn't sit still. She walked downstairs and put on a wash. She'd fold Candy's clothes. Then she'd iron. Then Norman would get up. Norman needed her. She could hear Candy pouring her cereal.

"Bye mom."

And she was gone. Tricia wondered if she'd go see Andrea or the other girls. Doug said he thought she was okay but what'd they talk about? Holidays in a week was a first-rate idea, Douglas you came through. Oh Candy, Candy.

Candy was walking to school fast. She was striding, cause she was still mad at Andrea. She was burnt up.

"Hey slow down, Candyass."

Candy kept going.

"Slow down, dopey."

She didn't. She pretended Andrea didn't exist. To heck with you you two-timing weasel. Andrea grabbed her arm.

"I said slow down."

"I heard you. You could wake the dead with your voice."

Andrea gave her a hard push.

"Who the hell do you think you are, Candy?"

Candy walked on fast, her teeth clenched and her fingers digging into her palms. I'll lambaste her, I will. Andrea grabbed her hard, turned her around and punched her in the belly.

"You want some more?"

Candy was scared. Andrea was bigger. Andrea didn't care what she did. Her fist was clenched.

"You dipsy doughnut. You turtle poop."

"What're you talkin about?"

"Vacuum lips."

"Shut up, Candy."

"Eyeballs. Dope bucket. Brain soup."

Andrea didn't know what to do.

"Cut it out, Candy."

"You cut it out, tongue lover."

"I just wanted to tell you something."

"You punched me, flamingo lips."

"Okay, insult me once more and I'll clean up the street with you."

"I've seen your house. You don't know what clean is. When'd you have your last bath? When Columbus discovered America?"

Candy didn't care what happened. And if she got punched she'd pull Andrea's hair. Andrea grabbed her shoulders and Candy punched her in the nose. And pulled her hair hard till she fell down on her knees. And walked away as fast as ever. Holy cow, she thought, now I'm in for it. Andrea's tough. Boy, that'll teach her. Don't mess with Candy.

CANDY WAS WIDE AWAKE IN CLASS AND PUT HER hand up like she was teacher's pet. She hated being that but she didn't care. Today she could be good or bad, she didn't care which. Even Andrea got an answer right and Mr. Lestock slumped down in his chair in shock.

"Is education really working? I'll have to write a letter to the education authorities saying that in spite of everything Andrea got a right answer. Thank you, Miss Patenaude, you've made my year. I'll come back to teach next year. Warn the Grade Sevens."

Gerald said, they already had Miss Vosberg so they'd been to purgatory already. Mr. Lestock said, "Thank you, Gerald, for those comforting thoughts." Nobody laughed. They were too nervous.

Candy said, "Freedom's just four days away." Candy didn't say things like that. Everyone held their breath.

"Ah yes," said Mr. Lestock, "in four days I'll be free of you all, even you, Miss McFarlane. And when did you learn to talk back? Perhaps there's hope for you after all."

At noon Andrea said, "All I wanted to tell

you, Candy flat chest, is I saw Ramon and Sam yesterday and he said to tell you to see him. I said, are you crazy, Ramon? She's such a mouse. He kissed me, I mean, really, and he said you tell Candy to see me and I'll kiss you again and you won't know which way's Monday. That's what he said and Sam said were you a scaredy cat and whyn't you phone her, so I told my message an I'm goin back for my kiss an why would he wanta see a wimp like you's beyond me, I mean you ain't in their class, goody goody numbnuts."

Candy heard Andrea talking but she didn't pay attention. She was going to see Ramon. She was going to see Sam. Everything was okay. She said thanks to Andrea and walked her home like they were old friends.

chapter 11

CANDY COOLED OUT THE NEXT DAY AND WHEN
the bell rang she went to the washroom, and
then out the back door of the school and down
the alley. She wasn't going to get trapped today.
She watched round the corner to make sure
Gerald had left and walked towards Broadway,
in her new super-fast way.

"Hey Candy, where's the fire?"

It was Kath, her friend in Grade Six, and she
owed Kath for her alibi and slowed down.

"Hi Candy, how come you're going my way?
Mr. Cowstock was okay today. How's Norman
anyway?"

"Crazy as ever. He dumps all his toys in his
jumper and clunks when he walks."

"He's a neat kid. I've been babysitting at
Cherry's. They've got two little girls, Sarah and
Martha, and they're okay, I even baked with
them. I go twice a week after school and some-

times at night, oh lookit that?"

There was a guy with his hand in a garbage can. He was old, with a scruffy beard and awful clothes. He pushed a bike with two big bags on it. They looked at him and looked away.

"That bum's so dirty."

"Yeah," said Candy, who'd seen him before in her own alley.

He scared her he was so rough looking, and there was something else she half saw. He was a failure.

"I hate him, don't you, Candy?"

"I guess."

"Let's get outa here. Hey, where you goin anyway?"

"I'm going to meet Andrea at the Red Robin."

"How can you talk to her? She's so mean. She's awful, like that bum. Does she hit you?"

"Not after yesterday. I knocked her on her ass."

"You? In your dreams you did. I'd love to see that. Hey, it's my corner. Nice to see ya. Give me a call?"

"Yeah. Sure. Bye Kath. See you."

Candy thought of when she used to go to Kath's. All they did was watch TV and talk about homework. Then she wondered if Andrea would already be at Sam's to get her kiss. When she turned down the alley it was empty. She walked to Sam's. Her heart was quiet. She told it to be quiet. She looked at it severely like it was a bad kid going to do something awful. She clenched her teeth a little to keep her heart in, then relaxed her mouth. She didn't want to look dumb if Ramon was there. Ramon. Her darn heart fluttered anyway. Shouldn'ta said his name. Shouldn'ta. Candy knocked on Sam's door and Ramon answered, in shorts and nothing on his chest. He was beautiful.

"Hey Candy, great, you come in."

The place was sure a mess, as bad as Mrs. Patenaude's.

"Where's Sam?"

"Red Robin, I go get her. Hey, c'mere."

When Candy walked over to Ramon he put his hands behind her head and kissed her on the lips. She let it happen. What could she do? Her legs went to jelly. She didn't kiss back. She hadn't any practice. It was something new. Way back in her head she knew she liked it. Ramon stepped back, grinned.

"I was to give kiss to Andrea. She didn't come. You got it. Okay?"

It was hard to say anything so she didn't.

"Okay, now I go get Sam. You wait. She'll want to talk to you. Bye, Candy."

"Bye, Ramon."

He left. Candy sat on a kitchen chair. Her heart was going to beat the band. Holy smoke, he kissed me, holy smoke. Candy shut her eyes and remembered one minute ago. She ran her forefinger on her lips, first the top, then the bottom, then she opened her eyes. What a mess. She had to do something. She was so excited she couldn't stay still, so she got up and cleaned the sink of junk, found some soap and started on the dishes, only it wasn't easy some of them were so crusted. She soaked them. She found a plastic bag and dumped in old pizza and cigarette butts and plate scrapings. Now I'm my mom, she thought as she scrubbed the plates clean. The shelves had to be washed before she put the cups away. Then there was the vacuuming. They had an old vacuum in a cupboard that was okay on the sort of brown rug with cigarette burn holes in it. She put beer bottles in their cases. She started defrosting the fridge, boiling the kettle first. There were lots of old towels to mop up the wet. Candy was a fast worker, just like her mom who was a hurricane cleaner, said her dad, who liked to leave a mess just to see how fast it disappeared. Ramon and Sam came back at five.

"Good God, look at this place," said Sam. "Candy, you do all this?"

"Don't look like where we live," said Ramon.

"You wanna be our cleaning lady? I'm just kiddin, I wanta talk to you."

"Yeah," said Ramon, and gave Candy a quick kiss on the cheek.

"You sure pretty, Candy."

"What time is it?"

"Five. Just after five."

"Oh no, I gotta go, sorry, or I'll get killed by my mom, sorry, sorry. Oh, the fridge isn't finished defrosting."

"Hey Candy, slow down, cantcha? Whatcha doin Saturday?

"Don't know. Nothing maybe."

"Come over'n see us in the afternoon."

"Okay, Sam. Bye."

Ramon grinned and waved his hand.

"See you, Candy."

"Bye."

Candy made it out of the basement apartment – she didn't know how. Her legs were jelly. They held her up. She walked out of the alley. She saw every step she took. When she turned the corner she stopped. She breathed in deep as she could and leaned against a fence and composed her mind. It didn't work. She was all over the place. She had to walk. She had to walk fast. She was late. So she walked fast away from Ramon's two kisses and Sam's surprise when she saw the place was cleaned up. When she opened the gate into her front yard Candy heard Gerald yell, "Hey dinglefoot," but she kept going into the house, where her mom said, "And where have you been, missy? It's after five. Were you with Andrea again?"

"I get my report card tomorrow. Hi Carboy, c'mere."

Carboy jumped for Candy who carried him into the living room away from her mom and dumped him on the floor and tickled him and he yelled, "Sum agla, Canny, sum agla."

"Want a spin, Carboy?"

And she picked him up, turned him upside down and spun in circles. He howled with pleasure.

"Candy! You'll drop him. Don't!"

Candy stopped spinning, put Carboy down and he walked like a drunk, laughing. Candy's mother laughed too and went back to her kitchen.

"Thanks, Carboy," Candy said quietly. "You got me outa a real hole."

When her dad got home he'd picked up maps for the trip and gave them to Candy so she could make plans about how to get to the coast. Tricia made chili for supper and said to herself, I didn't yell, I'm afraid if I yell she'll do whatever she wants. It's okay about her hair, that's okay, she's right, I have to control myself. I don't want to lose her, she's so nice. I've only got one daughter.

chapter 12

IT WAS SATURDAY MORNING, ANOTHER BEAUTIFUL day, and the sun came in a side window, where Sam and Ramon were finishing coffee.

"You think she'll come?"

"You kissed her, Ramon. She heard them bells. She'll come."

"We not so nice, Sam, using that girl."

"You want the money?"

"Sure."

"Okay then."

"Hey don't, Sam, don't put the cigarette ash in the cup."

Sam put the ash in the ashtray, grinned, picked up Ramon's coffee cup to rinse it.

"I know, it is funny, but I never had neat before. It's nice. My brothers were pigs."

"You wanna come visit Rhonda?"

"No, I don't go near Kilburn. It scares me. She's dumb eh. She can't stop the shoplifting."

"She can't stop. She takes everything, even guys' stuff and she ain't got no guy, and she can't wear it all. She steals stuff for me like these shoes. Imagine stealing shoes an they fit."

"She say why she does it?"

"No. She ain't like me. I talk, don't I?"

"What if that Candy comes?"

"I'll go straight to the bingo parlour. You drive her."

SAM TOOK THE BUS DOWN LORNE AND WALKED to Kilburn, gave her name, and they let her in and Rhonda was brought to the visitors' room and Sam gave her a Coke, a chocolate bar, a packet of cigs, and a couple of bucks. Rhonda took them.

"When you goin to trial?"

Rhonda shrugged.

"Did you want to get caught?"

"I dunno."

"Why do you steal stuff you can't use anyway?"

Rhonda shrugged.

Sam couldn't get her to talk. She looked sorta dead in the eyes. Sam was used to being in control these days, but Rhonda had gone out of sight. It troubled Sam but she said to hell with it, I got my own troubles.

RAMON TURNED ON THE TV AND WATCHED some talk show where women talked about boyfriends who cheated on them. Ramon graded the women and the good-looking guys, drank his second beer and fell asleep with the remote in his hand.

The door was open so Candy walked in, wearing jeans and a print blouse and her hair parted in the middle. She watched Ramon. She began memorizing him, legs sticking out in front, his head back and his mouth open, making small snoring noises, the dragon on his biceps, the maple leaf on his shoulder, his white teeth, lots of eyelashes like a girl, black hair with a curl over his T-shirt collar. Candy just looked, then looked around, no Sam, and the place was still neat. She tiptoed out and knocked at the door until Ramon woke up.

"Hi, Ramon."

"Candy, you came. Nice."

"How are you today?"

"Today, oh, good, sure, good. Wait, I wake up."

He went to the sink and splashed water on his face, lots of it, shook his head like a dog, got Candy wet.

"Oh, sorry."

Then he threw a handful of water at Candy.

"Hey."

"I dry you. Yes?"

Ramon went to the bathroom for a towel.

Candy poured a jug of water and when Ramon came back she poured it over him till he was soaked too.

"You dry me."

He gave her the towel. He sat on the chair. Candy had the towel. She started rubbing his hair. Holy smoke, she thought.

"Hey, harder, harder."

She rubbed hard. Yeah.

"Hey I'm wet here."

He pointed to his chest. Candy snapped him with the towel, which Ramon grabbed.

Candy said quickly, "How come you wanted to see me?"

"Oh yeah, Sam's gone to visit Rhonda, you know. In Kilburn. It's bad. She got caught. She is not smart."

"She scares me."

"You're a good student, yes, Sam told me."

"Yes."

Candy's heart was beating again. Being splashed by Ramon, drying his hair. She was ready to die. She took the remote and found a ball game. She watched. Ramon watched, puzzled. Ramon made coffee and brought her a cup. Their fingers touched. He added milk.

"Hey it's still clean, you see. I like it clean. I keep it clean."

He kissed the back of her neck.

"Don't."

She was scared. Something was going on in her belly, some excitement, some scariness. She wanted to be normal again.

"Where are you from Ramon?"

"Sixth Street."

"No, like I mean where were you born?"

"Here, Canada, like you."

"Oh, uh, where were your parents born?"

"Chile."

"That's the long thin country on the Pacific?"

"Yes. My parents had to leave or they would be killed by the bad man, Pinochet, and the good man was Allende."

"Why don't you live with your mom and dad?"

"Candy, Sam says, keep the nose on your face."

"Sorry, I'm sorry."

The more she talked the easier it became, not scary. Only if she stopped and looked at him she got all funny inside again.

"I'm Scottish, on my dad's side, only I don't know when anybody came from Scotland, and my mom is Norwegian but she doesn't even eat that fish or anything but her grandparents came from there."

Candy kept talking, only the phone rang and Ramon answered and said, "That was Sam. We meet her at Front Street Bingo. Okay? You got some time?"

"I got an hour left."

"Hey great, let's go, we take my car."

"You got a car?"

"Course I got a car."

It was a big old car with fins and a lot of rust and Ramon drove with one hand, the other arm resting on the car window in the sun. Candy figured why not. She was getting used to great things. She forgot she went to school. She forgot she had a family. She rolled her window down and rested her arm in the sun. That's who she was. She was so cool. She was in a car with Ramon. She wished they would just drive and drive. On Twentieth Street they pulled into the parking lot in front of a bingo parlour. She saw Sam inside playing, near the back.

"We watch her okay?"

Candy saw that Sam played seriously. When Sam looked up, ran her hand through her hair, Ramon drove around the back.

"Better to park here, out of the sun, yes. Sam will meet us here. I got to park. Hey you ask that guy to get her. Hey you know she got a new name for bingo? You play bingo?"

"No."

"Yeah, her bingo name, they know her, is Bingo, funny eh?"

Ramon touched Candy on the shoulder. She went in the back door. It was an office. A man was counting money.

"Hi," said Candy, "have you seen my friend, Bingo, her name is Bingo."

"You kidding me, honey?"

"No, she's out there. She was going to come home."

"One of those, eh? Got kids at home. Wait a sec. What's she look like?"

"Kinda big, with a black т-shirt."

When he left the room, Sam entered from outside, from the parking lot. "How come?" thought Candy. She took Candy to the car and Ramon walked in and out of the room and they drove down the alley, over to Twenty-second, Ramon watching in the rear-view mirror.

(chapter 13)

CANDY COULDN'T UNDERSTAND WHY SHE LIKED
the highway so much. It was flat as a pancake.
There were only towns and farms and a lot of
nothing. She could look out the side window
and see right to the edge of the world. She knew
the earth curved. It was a big ball like she taught
Carboy to kick. Now she saw where it ended, in
all directions. Her mom was in the back with
Carboy strapped in his car seat and already fast
asleep. Her dad liked driving so much he never
liked to stop until he reached his destination,
and today that was Calgary. How could anyone
like this trip, Candy wondered. There's nothing
to look at. They went past places like Cereal and
Strongfield where there was less than nothing.
What happened to all the people? Candy started counting curves and got to seven. She saw a
hawk on a telephone pole. She saw rows of fat
clouds with blue in between and got on her sail-

boat and let the wind drive her down the sky to the mountains. There was a car in front of them that looked like a space craft, only when her dad passed she saw it was two ten-speeds strapped on the top of a van.

"Going down into Drumheller, Candy," said her dad, "land of the dinosaurs."

It was a real hill with stripes, which were the geological history of the world said her dad, like rings on trees. He'd cut down a tree in the back-yard last year and showed her how you could tell it was fourteen years old. Her mom had to pee so they stopped at a Dairy Queen and got ice cream, and Candy walked Norman in the roaring heat. It came down on top and then bounced back off the cement. Norman loved ice cream and was a real goopy mess so she cleaned him up and they were off. Candy thought, I love it, nobody knows where I am, nobody. She thought of Sam and Ramon but her world had changed again and she was happy in the car. She'd learn to drive as soon as she could, in two years, that's all. The clouds were piling up like castles now. Carboy was talking a mile a minute to Candy who was now in the back seat looking after him.

"Canny, Canny, car."

"This is a real one, a real car."

"Car, car."

"See the field."

"Feel."

"And there's a cow."

"Cows, cows," he shouted.

They stayed in motel village in Calgary, upstairs in two rooms with a little kitchen. Tricia made a great meal of spaghetti and meat sauce and they all watched a movie on TV, an old one called *The Lady Vanishes*, which Candy thought was corny until nobody believed Iris that her friend was on the train, nobody at all until she couldn't even believe her own eyes. She was all alone. Then Gilbert helped and they solved the mystery. Boring Miss Froy was really a spy. When Candy went to sleep she had a dream, more a nightmare. She was being chased in her school only the corridors kept going like there was no outside and she didn't know who was chasing her, but she had to run and run until a girl loomed up and Candy ran down another corridor. She had to get out, only she ran into her own class. Everyone was there and she went straight out an open window only it was up in the air and she fell and fell and woke up, wide awake, and went back to sleep and it started again and she saw people she'd never seen in her life and then Andrea grinning with a huge face and something deep in the dream said stop and she stopped and told Andrea to get out of the way and the dream must have vanished and Candy slept in.

Next day they drove to Revelstoke, stopping

in the mountains wherever her mom wanted. She'd never seen her dad so nice to her mom, like listening to everything she said even and stopping wherever she wanted. That wasn't like him. Candy read the Accommodation Guide and picked a motel which had a pool and she took Carboy in with his horse life preserver and he splashed and laughed and ducked his head under once and came up spitting water all over Candy who laughed and got a mouthful that tasted of chlorine and spit back at him and he did it again and Candy said, "You're going to be a terror when you grow up, Carboy."

"Carboy."

"Terror."

"Tear."

"Water."

"Waher."

Candy forgot about Saskatoon, but even when she was happy there was a dark spot at the back of her mind. She talked, she read, she played with Carboy, she planned the next day with the maps, which her dad liked her doing, and she'd tell them things from the guidebooks, and when she went silent and watched the streams and rivers the dark spot returned. She was uneasy. Then it went away. The third night they made Vancouver and stayed with an aunt and uncle, Ethel and George, in a big house in Kitsilano and Candy walked down to Spanish

Banks and she'd never seen anything so beautiful in her life, the mountain, the ships, the water, downtown Vancouver tiny and white in the distance. When she got home her uncle had barbecued a salmon and Candy thought, yuck, it's fish. Her dad said try it, her mom said act your age, her uncle grinned, her aunt busied herself with serving rice. Carboy had shot under the table and was climbing up Candy's legs. She tried it, tried it again and figured there must be more than one kind of fish, and ate it and her uncle said she was now o-fish-ally a west coaster and her mom and dad laughed and laughed. Candy thought, they should hear Gerald.

One day they walked on the Capilano Suspension Bridge and Candy looked down and didn't look down again. She imagined falling to her death, but she liked walking on a bridge that shook. "Get your sea legs, Candy," her uncle said and she went back and forth twice and then looked down. It must be a mile down there. Her dad did everything in miles. No kilometres for him. "Heck, it's too hard to spell." Her mother was more up-to-date. "I married a French woman," her dad always said, kissing her mom right in front of everybody. They were weird.

Candy suddenly felt an echo of Ramon's kiss and the feeling lasted until she walked into the backyard with Carboy following. It had just rained. Big fat ugly grey slugs were sliming the sidewalk. Carboy got down on his hands and knees to look. "Oh yuck Canny," and Candy took him inside, swiped her aunt's box of salt and went out on a killing spree. She salted a slug and it shrivelled up.

"Me, me, me."

That was Carboy.

"Okay me, your turn."

He salted a slug and crinkled up his face as it shrivelled.

"Oooo," he said.

"My turn, Carboy."

And they did turns till the sidewalks were slug free, and her mom asked what were you doing? "Killing slugs."

"Oh no," said her uncle, "what will I put in my porridge now?" Candy scrunched up her face. Her aunt said he's only kidding.

"Sure, it's the worms I like for spaghetti."

The next day her dad was reading *StarPhoenix* newspapers he'd bought at a newsagent to catch up on the news. Candy picked one up to leaf through and on page seven she read of a robbery at the Front Street Bingo Parlour. Thieves got away with over seven thousand dollars. Police have leads and expect to make an arrest soon.

Candy's heart stopped. Her mind stopped. It couldn't hold everything in. She sat still. Could people tell looking at her she was a thief? Fear took over her mind, no, no, it was terror. She had never in her life been terrified. She remembered as a little girl being scared of nursery rhymes about the spider that sat down beside her, and the ogres in fairy tales. She remembered being afraid of her Grade Three teacher who talked of hell and there was a nightmare she used to have about a rat eating houses with people in them. But now she knew all that was nothing. Because they weren't real. They went away. This wouldn't go away. This was real. She was a thief. And Sam and Ramon, her friends, they had used her, they didn't care for her. They made her a thief. Oh God, I'm a thief. I'm going to jail. I'm going to jail! Whatever else they did on their holidays, Candy was terrified and when people talked to her they had to talk to her twice.

"What's wrong, Candy? Candy!"

"Nothing."

chapter 14

AFTER RAMON HAD DRIVEN AWAY FROM THE bingo parlour over to Twenty-second, with nobody in the rear-view mirror, they went over the University Bridge and towards home. Candy couldn't figure out what was going on and why Sam was in the office, not the bingo parlour, but she was in the place in the world she most wanted to be, with Sam and Ramon, but it was four so she said, "Drive me home, we've got to pack for tomorrow and I won't see you for three weeks. Do you like bingo, Sam? I didn't know you had another name, like Bingo is weird."

"My mom was a bingo nut, s'what she did all the time like when she wasn't home. But I like bingo yeah."

"Sure," said Ramon, "sometime you can win big. Here's your house Candy, you have a good ride with your mom and dad."

"See ya, guys."

Ramon pulled over on Tenth. Nobody was around. They couldn't wait. They opened the money bag and counted seven thousand dollars, and two hundred more. Wow. And it was so fast and so easy. Ramon put the money under the front seat and put garbage in front of it.

"You think she knows what we did?"

"Nah," said Sam, "she'd a said something."

"You think she that dumb?"

"She's a lot smarter'n me and you, but she don't know nothin."

"The guy saw her. If the cops get her?"

"She's straight, a cutie-pie, no record, and she's goin on holidays. Best front we ever had."

They drove to Sam's. They counted the money again. Sam started throwing her clothes in a big plastic bag, told Ramon to do the same. They oughta leave town. They got enough money. "Let's hit the road cause like if we spend fifty bucks in this town cops'll be all over us." Ramon said he better get rid of the car, cause he stole it.

"What!"

"I didn't think we should go on a robbery on foot."

"Ramon, you dipstick. I thought it was your car."

"For awhile."

Ramon drove downtown and left the car in a parking lot and they went to the bus depot and bought tickets for Regina, had a sandwich and were on the five o'clock bus. Ramon hated the prairie. He wanted the sea.

"What kind of country is this? Just flat everywhere. It takes away from a person."

Sam couldn't care one way or another. Ramon shut his eyes and was asleep in a minute. Sam put her arm on his knee. She liked touching him. She watched the fields go by in the sun. She'd grown up on a farm. She'd hated it. The memory made her sad but she had the zipper case with the money under her feet so she was okay. They'd done it. They'd done it! It was her plan from being with her mom playing bingo at the bingo parlour and watching where the money went.

WHEN ANDREA READ ABOUT THE ROBBERY next morning she went straight to Sam's place. She figured they'd done it. There was nobody home, but she knew the key was over the door and went in and poked around. Most of Sam's clothes were gone and all of Ramon's. There was no sign of Ramon, not a single one, not even a Rothmans king size. They done it, Andrea thought, they done it for sure and they left me out. Wonder where they went? It's not fair. I go to school and I'm really good for a week and whata I get? Left out! I wonder if Candy knows.

Ramon said he was sweet on Candy. Andrea walked fast over to Candy's and knocked but nobody was home, not even the big barking dog, and she remembered they were going on a trip.

GERALD WAS LONELY WITH CANDY AWAY. HE looked out his window and there was nothing there, only an empty house. He liked insulting her. He liked her insulting him. He watched her in class, so serious about her work, with that little frown between her eyebrows, her thick brown hair in braids or hanging down. He knew every costume she wore and liked her best in the pink sweater. That was his favourite. He liked school because he could watch Candy. Otherwise it was boring. He could do all his work so fast he never had homework and already wanted to be at university. He knew high school would be boring too. Candy was the smartest girl in Grade Eight, even if she had to work hard.

Why did she go with Sam? He didn't like Sam. She was too tough. She'd pushed him around in Grade Six and hit him because he made some smart remark. He hated Sam. He steered clear of her. At least she wasn't in school now. Or that dumb Andrea. Dumb bunny. Brain soup. Puke head. His invention left him. Candy wasn't there to get him going. He

watched the house. What else was there to do?
He decided he'd guard the house.

Next morning he saw Andrea at the house.
She even went round the back. Gerald decided
to be a spy, to follow Andrea. He was bored. It
was something to do. She went down the alley
and Gerald stayed on the street and watched her
crossing a block down. He got excited. He'd
never been a spy before. Andrea never looked
back because she didn't know she was in a
movie. She didn't know she had a shadow. She
walked to Broadway. He kept a block back. If he
was older he would have bought a newspaper
and pretended to read. What he did was pretend
to look in store windows. When Andrea turned
down Eleventh Gerald hid behind an elm tree,
then crossed the street and saw her go into a
basement apartment. She didn't live there so
who did? He waited and waited until Andrea
came out. She put something above the door
ledge. He watched Andrea leave and then
walked past the door of the place. There was no
noise and no light. He looked in the window,
took the key down where Andrea had left it and
went in, his heart beating. He was a spy for
Candy. There were cups and plates and food and
something had died in the fridge. There were a
few clothes in the closet, a sweater and jeans for
somebody really big. He thought, Samantha.
They're big enough for her, and ugly enough.

He looked at everything, like the towels and the hair in the shower and he figured two people, one brown-haired like Samantha and one black haired. He left, put the key where it belonged and the next day he watched Candy's, Andrea's and Sam's. A day later when he went to Sam's he saw police cars there. Gerald watched from behind a caragana hedge and heard the police talk. They knew about Sam. Somebody had seen her. They were there over an hour and left with bags full of stuff. Gerald let himself in again and all the clothes were gone and some cups and glasses and he thought they're taking fingerprints but he hadn't touched anything but a door. He was a spy. Would they find Candy's fingerprints? They wouldn't know whose they were. They'd know Sam's. She'd been in remand. I wish Candy'd come home. I want someone to talk to. I got so much stuff to tell her.

chapter 15

SAM AND RAMON GOT OFF THE BUS IN REGINA.

"Where we stay, Sam?"

"We got the cash we'll go first class, okay?"

"Sure. Okay."

They walked around. They looked at hotels. The Saskatchewan looked great, with its fancy blue canopy, so they decided to rent a room at the Hotel Saskatchewan. For the first time in their life they had money. They walked in and looked around. They'd never seen anything like it. Their running shoes sank in the rug.

"How will you pay for this, sir?"

"Money. Cash."

"You'll need to pay a night in advance then, sir."

"Okay. Sure."

Sam felt like dirt the way the guy spoke, as if they were nothing. Ramon peeled off five twenties and they got their key and carried their black plastic bags and a knapsack upstairs, unlocked the door, stepped in and jumped on the beds like little kids.

"We done it, Sam. We got here."

"Let's count it again, jus to make sure."

So they put the money in piles, the fifties, the twenties, the tens, the fives, and it still came to over seven thousand bucks, even after the bus and hotel. They looked at it. They pulled the drapes and looked down on Regina, then explored the room.

"Hey Sam, look, such a big bath."

Sam turned down the blankets and ran her hands on the sheets that didn't have a single wrinkle. Ramon turned on the TV.

"Not much on, eh, Sam?"

"Nah, it's crummy TV, but we can watch a movie later. C'mon, I'm starvin."

"What of the money? We should not leave it."

"I'll take it in the knapsack."

"Yes. Keep you warm."

They took the elevator down to the lobby. Sam saw the clerk looking at them. They walked into the restaurant but when they saw the chandeliers and people there in such good clothes, they knew they weren't dressed for it, even in their good duds, so they said to heck with this place and walked down the street and into the Copper Kettle where it was dark, especially in the bar, and they had steaks and a beer. They looked older than sixteen. They acted like it was nothing ordering a beer, like they did it everyday.

"I'm gonna propose a toast."

"What is that?"

"Well, like, okay. I propose a toast to our gettin away with it. C'mon, lift your glass and clink and drink. Hey, clink and drink. I shouldn't a quit English."

Ramon drank his beer. He felt good. A toast. He'd never heard of that. It was nice. He grinned at Sam, his white teeth shining in the dark. Sam got caught up in the grin and hunched her shoulders over the table and smiled with her mouth closed but her eyes open wide.

"I propose the toast."

"Good."

"I propose the toast to Sam-antha."

They touched glasses and drank. Sam got serious and ate her steak and chips. Ramon ordered two more beer. Sam looked around. There were four other people eating in the bar, four toque guys with wide pants, droopy pockets and running shoes. They ate with their toques on. They were okay. They weren't watching. Sam was ready to cry. Sam-antha. She'd worked hard against feeling things cause when she was little her mom hit her a lot and she remembered she'd rather be hit by her mom than be left alone but her mom hated her and her stepdad did too. Sam didn't know why she was so big. She just was. She wasn't a pig. She didn't eat a lot. When she started school she was big. Hey fat ass. Girls were worst. She hated pretty girls. She hated them. Hey tub. Her mom didn't care what she looked like so she looked awful. In Grade Five she had to wear sweatpants to school. "I ain't made a money Sammy, just get your butt to school and keep outa my hair." In Grade Six when a girl was making fun of her she swung her big arm and knocked her down real hard. There was a hush in the playground. The girl told on Samantha and the principal talked to her mother who said, "What can I do? She's unruly." They kept her on probation and when she belted another girl who called her a retard and then sat on her till she cried, she got sent to special ed as a problem child. They treated her dumb so she became dumb. To hell with them. That's where she met Rhonda. Rhonda hardly ever talked and Sam felt okay with her cause Rhonda was worse off than her, she never knew why, so they became friends.

Ramon smiled at her. She never believed Ramon would like her. Nobody liked her. Nobody messed with her either. Nobody liked her, but they didn't make fun of her anymore. She didn't know when it happened, but people didn't act like she was a retard anymore. She was big. She would never get a guy. A guy wouldn't like her. She was too big. Maybe a big guy. She'd seen big guys. But nobody as beautiful as Ramon. She didn't even dream of him that way. I ain't gonna get hurt no more. No way. Keep it cool, keep it down. Robbing, that's okay. She didn't care if she got caught. It was her life. Nobody was calling her a tub of lard. She never met those stuck-up girls now. Except Candy. When she met Candy she figured she'd get her own back, make her front the robbery, get back at all those rotten girls. Candy was one of them. She did good in school. Then Sam remembered Candy phoned her about the cellphones, to warn her. She said I was smart. Ah so what, so what? To hell with her.

"Hey, Sam, hello, hello."

"Sorry, I was thinkin. What we'll do tomorrow cause we should get outa Saskatchewan. We both got records so they'll go for us. You see the way that guy at the hotel looked at us, like dirt, like dirt. Think he phoned the cops?"

"Toast. To beer. I like toast."

"We oughta get some fancy duds tomorrow."

"Sure."

"An rent a car an get outa town so they won't get us."

"I do not have a licence."

"But you drive a car, Ramon."

"I can drive. I can steal one. I steal many cars. Never been caught. I cannot buy one."

They walked around Regina in the hot July night. It was beautiful. They felt that. The colour was very muted, very warm. They had a room in this great hotel. They had money in Sam's knapsack, more money than they ever had, a lot better than crummy welfare.

"Hey," said Ramon, "bingo, a toast to bingo."

They raised invisible beer bottles and pretended to drink. When they went into the lobby of the Saskatchewan Sam looked at the room guy because she was scared of him. He was watching them. She saw that. Ramon got on the elevator but Sam didn't. She watched the guy from around a column. He was phoning someone. She got on the next elevator and grabbed Ramon when he was going to unlock the door.

"Lissen. There's no TV on. We left it on."

"Oh yeah."

"We gotta get outa here, Ramon. I think maybe it's cops."

Ramon followed Sam. She was smarter than he was. He didn't care if the cops got his stuff. He didn't care about owning things. He liked to steal money. He dreamed of a car, of fancy clothes, of things he'd seen in movies, but he didn't really care. He didn't need things. He'd never had them. When Sam started walking down the stairs he did too. Fast. They left their stuff behind. Okay, how could they get past that room guy?

"He's told on us, we need a suitcase, yknow, to look like everybody else."

A suitcase, thought Ramon. I never think of that. Sam raised her hand to say stop. Ramon had to go and went into the men's. Sam waited by the pillar until four guys who must have been jocks started to get rooms. They had jackets that said Clippers and caps on with their peaks backwards. "Now," said Sam, "act natural," and they walked past the desk and out the door. The guy saw them at the last moment but he was tied up and they got in a cab and drove out Albert to a motel. Sam said she needed a coffee so they crossed Albert and sat in a McDonald's.

"Hey, the big M."

"That's for money."

Cop cars pulled up to the motel where they'd been dropped off.

"Why are they there?"

"They're lookin for us."

The cop cars went down to the next motel. Sam and Ramon waited till they left and climbed into an empty Loraas bin. It was half full of large black garbage bags.

"We gotta get outa here before the garbage in the morning."

"It do not smell too bad."

"It ain't the Hotel Saskatchewan."

Sam slept with her head on the money. Before he went to sleep Ramon asked, "How come we had the coffee? Did you know the cops come?" Sam said she didn't trust anybody.

"How bout me?" asked Ramon. "I trust you, we done it together."

"You ever told on anybody, Ramon?"

"No, no, you mean to cops? No, no, never do that. Never. My parents had bad times with police. They know, never talk to cops."

"You can lay your head on my belly to sleep if you wanna."

"Okay."

They were tired from beer. They were asleep in no time.

chapter 16

IT DIDN'T MATTER WHERE SHE WAS, CANDY was black inside. She was standing by Osoyoos Lake. It was hot as can be, the sun pouring down. Candy went swimming. First she walked and walked till the water got up to her belly and then she swam. She did the deadman's float and looked at the blue sky. She did a slow crawl and could see how the world curved. Even the lake was curved. It was dead still. The waves were an inch high. It was perfect. But Candy couldn't push the future away from her. She was defenceless. It was coming. Doom was coming. Prison was coming. She was a thief. It wasn't fair! She didn't know they'd steal. They'll get caught, she knew it, cause everyone knew they were bad.

She walked out of the water and tugged the bottom of her bathing suit. Her dad was barbecuing. You could rent a barbecue from the motel.

She sat on a lawn chair looking at paradise. That's what her mom called it. She'd seen her dad kiss her mom last night when they didn't know she was looking. They're so old, she thought. Then she thought about Ramon and she knew for sure his kiss was a lie. The kiss was a trick. It's cause she's cute. Cute. She hated the word. She was cute so nobody would think she was bad. It was all a trick. It was hard for Candy to face it. Sam must hate me, to use me like that, like stealing the cellphone. That was a test. Boy, am I a jerk. I'm a jerk. Was Andrea in on it? Or is she a jerk too? Candy thought of just an ordinary day, like a boring day, like her mom nagging, or Gerald making fun of her or Murphy wanting a walk. She wanted to be in the middle of a really boring day. But the world had changed. It didn't matter what she wanted. It didn't matter where she lived. It didn't matter that supper was barbecued ribs and corn on the cob and ice cream pie. It didn't matter that her mom was nice as pie. She knew what was coming. She'd go to jail. Like Rhonda. And every mile they drove home brought her closer to disaster.

GERALD DIDN'T HAVE ANYTHING TO DO. THERE was no spying anymore. He walked by Sam's place each day. He even watched Andrea's house, and sat in the window looking at Candy's house. Nothing ever went on, not for four days. He wondered where Sam and Ramon had gone. Why weren't they caught? He talked to kids from class. They were surprised he talked to them. Gerald was such an egghead he didn't talk to anybody except Candy. He was soft on her. Everybody knew that – except Candy. Gerald learned Ramon had a car, a blue Cavalier. Nobody'd seen anybody. He went to the bingo hall and walked around and saw the office where they stole the money. Its door was open. Gerald tried to reconstruct the crime. How could they do it? They both look like losers, they both look like crooks. Gerald thought and thought but he got nowhere. He didn't have an answer.

"Hey kid, whatcha doin?"

"Nothing."

"Yeah, well get outta here."

"I've not done anything wrong, sir."

"This place got robbed, yknow."

"I know, I was wondering how it was done."

"Well I'll tell you, cause I was the guy, I was the guy that was robbed."

"Is that right, sir?"

"How they did it was this. Some little girl, like innocent as new blown snow, she came in and says, can you get this lady, like her kids are waiting, and her name, what a bonehead I was, her name is Bingo. So, I'm a nice guy, I was a nice guy, I say sure, walk into the bingo parlour, come back, she's gone, the money's gone and I'm the schmuck of the month, people making fun of me ever since and yknow what I did wrong? I believed in a person. Never again. Hey, why're you here? What's your interest? Are you a crook?"

"I certainly am not. It must have been terrible for you."

"Yeah, how old are you?"

"Fourteen."

"You remind me of that girl, real polite, real polite, like you'd be her father. So what's your angle, kid?"

"I am fascinated by crime, like a person who reads detective novels."

"I gotta go to work, kid, and I see your face here again I'll phone the cops. You got it?"

Gerald left and walked down Twentieth Street, and he knew sure as shooting it was Candy. His heart sank. He walked over the traffic bridge. He thought, she could not have done it. She could not have known. That Sam is duplicitous. You can't trust Sam as far as you could throw her.

SAM WOKE UP SUDDENLY EARLY NEXT MORNING. Something was wrong. She was sweating like mad. It was like an oven in the Loraas bin. She was nervous. Something was wrong. She eased away from Ramon and opened the lid and looked out, real careful. She gave Ramon a kick. It was real silent out. There were a few cars going by on Albert. Could they get out without being seen?

"C'mon, we gotta be fast."

Sam pushed the lid back and climbed out. There they were, two guys watching her, ball caps, jeans, boots, one with long black hair and glasses. Ramon climbed out, still dead tired.

"What're you lookin at anyway?"

The guys made no sign they heard her.

"You ain't ever been poor?"

Ramon looked at Sam, then dove back in the bin for the knapsack. They walked into the motel and there was no one at the desk. They had to go to the bathroom and they washed up and then checked the back door and the guys were there and there was a guy out front right by the door in the shade so they went in a room that had been just cleaned and climbed out a side window. They saw the guy out front meet his girl who drove him away. The other two guys got in a truck and drove off.

"Boy, am I jumpy."

"Good to be careful," said Ramon.

They went for coffee, waited till Wal-Mart opened at nine and bought stuff, like Ramon bought new jeans and two bright shirts, a pair of black dress shoes and new runners and Sam bought a dress she figured she looked like an elephant in and a net sweater, three new blouses, and dress shoes her feet hated. Then they bought a nice suitcase and Ramon picked out a necklace for Sam and she bought dark glasses for him and a sun hat. They paid in cash, walked out with their loot in the suitcase and the backpack and Ramon was feeling so good he walked around back of the store where a guy left his green Buick running while he went in to get his kid and Ramon swiped it and Sam got in and they were gone, west on Trans-Canada 1.

"Not so fast, don't get caught."

Samantha pushed a button and the roof pulled back and the sun and wind blew on them and they felt free all the way to Moose Jaw where Ramon parked the car in a mall parking lot in the middle of other cars.

"They would catch us. I'll steal another one."

There was an old Ford half-ton with its window a bit down in the lot so Ramon took a coat hanger from Sam's new clothes and pulled up the lock and they climbed in and he stuck wires together.

"It is a thing I am best at."

And they were away on the highway going west in the full sun. They had lunch at a gas station on the highway at Gull Lake. Ramon parked the half-ton behind a semi. Two

Mounties came in for coffee. Sam caught Ramon's leg between her own when he tried to get up. She frowned at him. They ate slowly. They tried not to look at the Mounties. Ramon was ready to make a run for it. Sam caught him with her eyes. He couldn't eat the chips. He'd gag. Sam got steely tough, fed Ramon a chip like a game, and he ate it. The Mounties waved at the owner and left. The semi had gone but they hadn't spotted the half-ton. Ramon wanted to drive like a maniac to get to Alberta but the traffic was so heavy he had to drive like everyone else.

"They won't catch us," said Sam, "cause they can't even see us in all the traffic."

chapter 17

CANDY AND HER FAMILY STOPPED IN CALGARY
for two days to visit their dad's friends from university. It was a neat house. It was full of paint-
ings and was very dark with wood around doors
and windows and they ate outdoors on a patio
under an apple tree. Tricia watched Candy.
Something was wrong. Candy was polite and
helpful. She couldn't have been nicer. She
learned to fill the dishwasher the right way. She
let her mom teach her to iron a sheet. She
helped their friend Wanda weed the garden and
pick lettuce and beets. Tricia suddenly wanted
her to talk back, to say no. She was perfect. It
bothered Tricia – that wasn't the Candy she
knew, the stubborn one, the disobedient one,
and she was lonely for that Candy. The new one
was like a grown-up, like a perfect kid, like a
robot, that's it, she's a robot. There must be
something wrong.

When Candy took Norman around the Heritage Village she forgot the future. There were so many words to teach him. She carried him in her arms and said, "Window."

"Winow."

"Fan."

"Fan."

"Porch."

"Porsh."

"Statue."

"Chew."

Then they ran on the lawn and Candy caught Carboy – then he caught her and she fell down and he jumped on her and knocked out her breath. When she got up she laughed and laughed. So did Carboy. Until they drove back to their friends' house when she suddenly remembered and almost puked. She opened the window. She was pale.

"Are you okay, Candy?"

"I don't feel very good."

"What's wrong?"

"Dunno."

She couldn't tell her mom and dad. She couldn't tell them. It was a secret. It was her own secret shame. Then she thought, they'll know when it becomes public. I'm doomed. But she couldn't tell.

TRICIA AND DOUG HAD GONE FOR COFFEE IN downtown Calgary to talk about Candy.

"I just don't understand, Trish. She usually laughs so hard at my corny jokes. Now it's like she doesn't hear me. I can't stand it."

"I know, I know. What bothers me – and this is really strange, I can hardly believe it's me talking – she's too good, too polite. Can you believe that?"

They skimmed the tops off their *caffe lattes* and sat in silence. They didn't know what to say.

"I can't stand it."

"She was okay when we started, Doug."

"She was, sure, and then she got introverted in Vancouver, yes, Vancouver. I don't know why. Do you, Trish?"

"Maybe she's homesick."

"She was so happy to travel, reading maps, looking after Norman."

"Lucky we've got Norman. She's herself with him."

"I can't stand it."

RAMON DITCHED THE STOLEN HALF TON IN A CAR park in Calgary, and they decided it was dumb to steal another one. They'd get caught for something dumb. They'd take taxis. Sam said they shouldn't stay in good hotels. They'd stick out. They'd get caught. So they stayed in motel village, like Candy had, and watched TV and once Sam kissed Ramon but he wasn't interested. She hated herself. She went for a walk. She wanted a drink but the bar asked for ID. They counted their money every night – but what could they do with it? They couldn't even have a drink. It was worse than Saskatoon when they were broke. Ramon said, "To hell, we not spending money." Sam said, "What if you loved me," and bit her tongue. Ramon said, "I don't love girls." Sam said, "What!" Ramon said, "I did not plan that. It just happen. I'm sorry. You're great. You're so smart. I like you." "What about Candy?" "I kiss her for you. You're the best girl I know. I cannot do what I cannot do. I kiss you." He did, a real one. "That is it. Don't be mad, Samantha. I cannot help it. It's a thing."

"Okay," said Sam, "okay, okay, okay, but I want a drink, dammit. I want a drink. We got all this money and I can't have a drink. I can smoke my brains out but we got a fortune. I want a drink."

"Okay, okay, I go get you one!"

Ramon took a cab to Sixteenth. He figured if I'm going to steal do it a long way from home. He was too young to buy booze. He didn't know anyone. He had to steal it. He watched till six people went in and followed and took a bottle of rye and a bottle of rum fast, put them in his knapsack and walked out but a bell rang when he passed the pillars by the exit and he ran. He always ran. He knew about getaways. Only he ran into a young guy with a shaved head selling flowers who fell down and Ramon fell over him, hitting his head on a car fender so he was dazed and somebody grabbed him and a cop was there when he looked up.

"What's your name, kid?"

"Walter."

But his wallet had fallen out and the cop looked at it.

"It says Ramon Moretta here."

Ramon thought fast. They got me. I gotta protect Sam. He put his hand in his jeans pocket. The motel key was there. He had to ditch it or they'd get Sam, and the money too. He saw the other cop on a cellphone in the car. Ramon coughed like he was hurt bad, doubled up and slipped the key under a car. No one heard it drop because a van was pulling away and he was coughing loud.

"Ramon, you're wanted for robbery in Saskatoon."

"That's not true."

"You're from Saskatoon?"

"Yes."

"How'd you get to Calgary?"

"Bus."

"Where'd you get the money?"

"It not so much. Welfare."

"Where's Samantha Didick?"

"Who?"

"The girl who helped you rob the bingo parlour."

"How they know I do it?"

Ramon was suddenly afraid. The car he'd hid the key under pulled away.

"Take me to station, I talk to you there."

"Climb in, kid."

Ramon got in the back of the car with one cop while the other went back into the liquor store.

"What is he doing?"

"Shut your face."

The cop came back out with a dozen beer, stopped, bent over and picked up the key. It had a tag on it. Ramon felt like a dope to leave the tag on.

"Scotchman's Motel. This your key, Ramon?"

"Never see it before."

"Let's drive on over."

Samantha had gotten nervous that Ramon wasn't back and was sitting at Arby's where she could watch the motel door. The cops pulled up with Ramon. Sam was now entirely alive. She was excited. She saw them go in the office. She saw the clerk nod. They walked down to the motel door on the second floor. Sam grinned. She'd learned from Ramon. She'd taken the money with her. I'll go to the coast, she thought. I'll take a plane. They ain't gettin me. I'll meet a big guy. She paid for her coffee and walked out the door.

"Samantha Didick, you're under arrest for robbery."

She had no feelings. They put handcuffs on her. She was bigger than the cop. There was only one car. They sat her in the back, Ramon in the front. He said quickly as they passed, "The cleaning lady, she knows where you go for coffee."

"No talking, you two."

Sam thought, I'm gonna be famous, I stole seven big ones. Rhonda'll wet her pants. I'll be famous. Yeah, yeah, yeah. She didn't mind jail. She'd been in Kilburn, in remand. She was big. She was tough. She'd take charge. Not like school, not like school. Ramon was scared. He'd been in remand. He hated it. You were cooped up. Other guys were tougher. He was great on the street. He was king of Broadway. In jail he was nothing, nothing at all.

CANDY WAS ON HER WAY HOME. SHE WATCHED each town passing, little towns that were hardly alive, Richdale, Chinook, Sibbald, and each town was like a nail driven into her heart. There was no way to stop. She was trapped in the car.

It was like doom. The car went on and on. Marengo, Flaxcombe, McGee. They stopped for lunch at Kindersley. The heat was like a blanket when they walked across the parking lot. It was like fire. Zealandia, Harris, Delisle. They were coming closer and closer. Carboy was asleep. So was her mom. Candy was wide awake. She remembered the last time they came to Saskatoon after a trip to the Coast. She loved it. Past the grain terminal, the little houses, a confectionery, trees everywhere, over the iron bridge, the excitement of coming home, with the fridge breathing and getting the dang dog and asking Carboy if he was happy. She loved coming home. Now she was terrified. What would she find? Would she go to jail? It used to be so nice. Now it was just awful.

chapter 18

CANDY LOOKED OUT THE WINDOW. SHE SAW Gerald on his front step, like he was waiting for her. She stepped back out of sight. She watched, then her eyes went blank. She wasn't looking at anything. She'd gone back inside. She didn't know she looked crestfallen. Her dad did.

"You okay, Candy? Candy? Hello, hello. Father beaming in to daughter captured by aliens."

"Oh, hi dad."

"What's wrong, Candy?"

"Nothin."

"You keep looking into space. See any funny people yet?"

She should have laughed at that. That's how Doug and Candy got along. She was supposed to laugh.

"Candy, when I say something funny you laugh, okay?"

She just looked out the window. She'd never been so low. She watched herself. I've never been so low. Go away, dad. Leave me alone, she thought, I want to be sad. I want to feel crummy. Sad and bad and lowdown and alone. She felt her dad's arms around her. He was warm. He was big. She started to cry. She saw it was herself who was crying. Leave me alone, dad. He turned her around and held her from the front. He was wearing one of the cotton shirts she liked. She cried and she cried. He said, "Shh, it's okay, Candy, it's okay, it's okay." She saw herself leaking, like a roof in a big rain. She thought that. I'm the garage roof that leaks. Dad is fixing it. He held her tighter. She felt his hand patting her back like he did when she was really little. She thought, I'm a robber and a crook. I'm grown up and tough. I know Sam and that damn Ramon and I've been betrayed, and she kept crying. She couldn't turn it off. She watched herself cry. It's a crying jag. I've held it in for so long. I'm a crook, I'm going to jail, so it's okay to cry, let it all out. Her dad was looking at her. He wiped her eyes.

"It's a clean hanky, sweet Candy."

That was his old name for her. She saw her mom through the tears like a blurry mom. She saw her dad shake his head and her mom vanished – like in a movie, thought Candy. My dad's the director. I'm the crier. She ran out of tears and quit crying. There's no water left inside me, she thought, I ran out of water.

"You okay, Candy?"

"Sure."

She'd said a word out loud. Well, she was okay, she'd been through a lot. She could even talk. Boy, was she strong.

"I'm okay, dad."

"What's wrong?"

"I'm okay, dad."

"Gerald's over there like a faithful dog."

"Huh."

"I don't know what's wrong with you, Candy, and I'm Dr. Freud at your service, my liddle lady, so vat I think is go see that unhappy boy who spends all his time looking at you. Now Gerald is very smart, yes? So vy does he want such a damp girl?"

Her dad was really trying.

"I'll go say hello. Okay."

"Okay."

Her dad waited at the door. Candy waited by the window till he left. She wanted to be alone. That's all. She didn't want anyone to push her. She sat on her dad's chair. She forgot about Gerald. Not thinking of anything. That's what she was doing, not thinking, growing small, growing invisible. No one will see me, I'm right here and I'm outa here. Something was wrong. She came out of her reverie. Knocking, that was it. She got to her feet and went to the door.

"Hi Candy."

"Oh, Gerald, it's you."

"I missed you."

"Oh."

"Nobody to insult, dope bucket."

"Oh."

"Candy? Candy? Come on out? I want to talk."

They walked across the street and sat on Gerald's porch. He didn't do any more insults. He'd never seen Candy sad. She must know about the robbery. It was her, I'm sure. What can I say to her?

"Where's Murphy?"

"My dad'll get him first thing tomorrow."

"Our cat has taken over your yard."

"I saw him. He's big."

"The weather was very nice."

Candy was looking a long way away. Gerald decided to jump in.

"Did you hear that Sam and Ramon are in Kilburn waiting for a trial for robbery?"

"No."

"They were caught in Calgary and are charged with robbing the Front Street Bingo Parlour of over seven thousand dollars. It's serious because they both have priors. I asked my dad. He said they're too young for prison but they'll do time in Kilburn and if they don't have parents that are appropriate they'll go to foster homes."

Candy tried to say that's awful, but she swallowed her words. She couldn't talk.

"Candy."

"Yes."

"There was a preliminary. I went."

"Oh."

"The Crown counsel asked about a third person."

Candy felt like she was in the car again. She wasn't in control. She was just going where everything took her.

"They didn't say who."

"Oh."

"Guy at the Bingo Parlor said a nice girl fronted for them and tricked him."

"Who?"

"They don't know. Sam and Ramon didn't say."

"Oh. I should go see Sam."

"Don't."

"Why?"

"Just don't do that, Candy."

"Bye Gerald."

He wanted to say he'd be there for her. He wanted to tell her he'd been a detective. He wanted to say how smart he was to figure it all out. He knew more than the cops. He wanted to say he was happy she was home. He wanted to say he watched her all the time. But he didn't. He just blundered out the story. But he had to tell it. She had to know. He wanted to tell her he watched her all the time. What is the point of being as intelligent as I am, what is the point of having the best marks, what is the point of doing better than everyone, of looking down on others, what is the point of being me if I can't tell Candy anything important? I want to tell her I watch her all the time. Maybe she'd hate me then. Maybe she'd never insult me again. Maybe in my whole life I'd never kiss her or feel her breast. Gerald watched Candy go into her house. She walked like she was half dead, like she was smaller. She wasn't Candy. What could he do?

Candy went into the bathroom at home. Her mom and dad were in the kitchen. Maybe I'm okay. They didn't tell. I don't feel okay. She took one of her mom's sleeping pills and went to bed. She had to knock herself out. She couldn't live with her own mind. When she woke the next morning she knew she'd had bad dreams but she couldn't remember anything. The sun was pouring into the bedroom. Candy stretched and felt good. Then she had to take a pee. There it is, she thought, like being in a car, you're not master of yourself. She heard Murphy barking in the yard and saw Carboy chasing him.

chapter 19

SAM KNEW ABOUT BEING IN KILBURN. DO everything you're told. Keep the rules. Be nice and say you're sorry a whole lot, show how sorry you are for what you did. Be penitent. She learned that word from a lady who talked to her, a counsellor.

"Samantha, are you angry?"

Sam had to think fast for every question. She knew she couldn't pretend to be nice as pretty girls, nice as Candy.

"Sometimes I get mad."

"What about?"

"Well, about being so big, like kids always made fun of me. You're really neat yknow, like a good size, but me, like it doesn't matter so much now but I got mad when they made fun of me there."

"Who?"

"Girls, in school, girls."

"Are you still mad?"

"I'm okay now."

I'll tell her about my mom and that bugger Roy the stepdad from hell. She's got it in that file anyway.

"My mom didn't wanta have me. She wasn't married and then there was this guy she married, I mean a lot later, when I was big enough, and he, well, you know, he, he screwed me, you know that? You got that down in your file already."

"Yes, Samantha."

"So, would you be angry?"

"Tell me about school."

"Would you be angry?"

"You didn't do well in school."

She's that kind, thought Sam, control freak, so I gotta cool it. What's she already know?

"They put me in dumb schools so I got dumb. I'm not dumb but they treated me dumb."

"Do you always blame others for your failures?"

Gotta watch my step. She's a killer lady. Shoulda known by her suit with all those legs showing. I'd die to have legs like that.

"When you're little what can you do? I mean, you can't figure things out like why're you big and why's your mom like she is but I'm okay now. I don't do that anymore. I can make my own way."

"What if you're convicted?"

"I can do time."

"Will you blame anyone?"

"Like who?"

"I don't know."

"Me neither. Like who'd I blame?"

"I don't know."

"Me neither."

"What will you do for a living?"

"I wanta take a course at Kelsey in motor mechanics cause I like motorcycles and I'm good at fixing engines already and I can do that."

Sam had never fixed an engine in her life, but she had to say something and she figured she'd meet some great guys on motorcycles. That's where she'd seen big guys.

"Thank you, Samantha. I wish you well."

"Thanks, Miss Morrison, and have a nice day."

SAM HAD BEEN WATCHING RHONDA. SHE DIDN'T talk to anybody. At meals she smashed her cutlery on her plate. Her eyes looked like knives to cut into you. Her mouth was set and when she opened it she sneered. Sam thought she was like an animal. At gym Rhonda grabbed the basketball and hucked it hard as she could at the male coach, who kind of caught it turning away and drilled it back to Rhonda who then threw it overhand as hard as she could and he pulled back and it hit a girl on the nose and blood spurted out. It was broke. On the way back to their rooms Sam put her arm around Rhonda hard and said, "You throw that ball at me I'll break your neck. Understand? Say yeah. Say it." She hugged tighter. Rhonda looked at her like she hated her. "Say yeah." Rhonda wouldn't talk. She just looked like she wanted to kill Sam, who let her go. "Hey, we were friends, Rhon." She walked off. Sam recognized hatred. She'd lived it herself. Hatred. For years. She never felt it now. Robbing made her feel easy, relaxed, good. She liked robbing. But she'd loved that hatred. She remembered. After her stepdad screwed her and her mom wouldn't believe it. She'd felt hatred. Now too, again. Hatred. For him, Roy, all over again. Roy's the boy, he used to say, his mouth smelling like an ashtray. Sam hadn't smoked in Kilburn. She decided she had to be tough as nails. So give something up. Everybody smoked. Not her. She knew how to look like Rhonda did. Look right through people, look at them like worms. Look at them like teachers looked at her.

When she had her second counselling session Miss Morrison asked about Rhonda.

"Do you talk to her very much?"

"Nope."

"Why's she so mad, do you think?"

"She don't talk to me."

"You were her friend."

"We never talked much. Sumpen's made her mad."

"If she had a gun do you think she'd kill us?"

"Yeah."

"And you?"

"I don't hate nobody."

"Your stepdad? You broke his jaw."

"That's dead and gone. I'm done with that."

At lunch Rhonda threw a plate against the wall and kneed one of the attendants in the balls and they dragged her off.

WHEN RAMON WAS QUESTIONED BY THE counsellor, he said he'd done the robbery. He didn't say that right away. It took ten minutes.

"Who did it with you?"

Ramon was caught. He had to say Sam. He didn't have to say Candy. He shouldn't say anything. He was scared. She'd said a confession would go easier. But he hated to tell a cop anything, cause he remembered what his parents said about Chile. Police were the enemy.

"Are you a counsellor?"

"I'm a policewoman. We've got the money, your fingerprints on the carrying case. We know it's you and Samantha. It was in her possession. Who's the third person?"

You don't turn anyone over. You don't tell cops. Never. He said, "Samantha."

"And the pretty girl?"

"Huh?"

He wouldn't say. You don't tell cops. He wanted Samantha to like him. You don't tell cops.

RHONDA FELT FULL OF POWER. SHE LIKED IT. They grabbed her, and hit her hard in the belly because she kneed one of them. Hit me, you shits, hit me. She was thrown in her room, hit her head on the end of the bed. It hurt. She liked it. She liked it cause it made her mad. She'd break that guy's finger with the basketball. She'd break everything. She pulled the sheet off her bed and tied it tight as could be round her neck and pulled but there was nothing to hang herself on. It was no good, but she tore the sheet up. She could do that. She smashed the wooden drawers. I'll break everything. Sam won't break. I'd need a knife or a club or a gun. She could break me like a drawer. I'll make her, I'll make her smash me. I'll smash that fairy Ramon. That'll do her. Yeah. Wish I had a gun. Wish I had a knife. I got nails. I'll carve that Ramon in the corridor. Pretty boy, I'll get him. Then Sam'll kill me.

chapter 20

TWO DAYS LATER AS THEY PASSED IN THE corridor Rhonda attacked Ramon with her fingernails. She scratched them down his face and he cried out but turned his hips so her knee hit his thigh and he slugged her in the stomach, once, twice, till she let go and he swung her round, shoved her into the wall and hit her once in the kidney before the staff came and tore him away. They eased back from Rhonda until two women staff took her away. She was smiling. Ramon was a lamb, Rhonda was a lion. A little mousy girl saw it all and said, "Rhonda started it and the guy jus defended hisself cause she's, she's so, uh, scary and uh."

Rhonda was isolated in her room. Psychiatric counselling had no response from her. She spoke to no one. They talked of her potential anti-social behaviour, her sudden uncontrollable rages. Sam said at lunch to two girls at her table that shoplifting was as good as it got with Rhonda, and eating faster than anyone alive and pouring on so much ketchup you couldn't find the fries.

"Maybe she's a bloodsucker."

"Yeah, a potato vampire."

"She sure wanted Ramon's blood."

"You sweet on him, Sam?"

Sam looked at the girl who shut up, but the other one talked.

"He punched her in the baby. You didn't know she's knocked up?"

"How do you know?"

"I'm ina next room. I hear her gettin sick in the morning."

"That's it?"

"Yeah."

"Where'd you get your doctor's degree?"

"Same place as you, Sam, on the street."

CANDY FIGURED IF SHE WAS DONE FOR WHY worry. If it happens it happens. She was trying to keep her fear down. Every night in bed she looked it in the eye. When she was littler she'd had awful nightmares. A giant bug chased her and she'd wake up screaming. Her dad rushed in, "Candy, Candy," and held her and asked what's wrong and she told of the giant insect. He said, "Okay, listen, here's what you should do. Go back to sleep and when the bug comes you count its legs." Next morning Candy said sixty-four. "Pardon," said her mom. "The bug that attacked me in my sleep had sixty-four legs." The bug never came into her mind again. So she figured if she looked fear in the eye she'd conquer it. And it sorta worked. Only she knew the bug wasn't real and the robbery was. Still she was able to walk Murphy and play rambunctious games with Carboy.

She never walked Murphy near Andrea's. She didn't want to meet anybody, except Gerald. He was always there. Only no insults now. Candy knew he knew she was at the robbery. She didn't know how, but he knew. Only he never said anything. And he would never tell on her. She was certain. One day when they were walking Murphy they were talking all the time but they weren't saying anything only they were so engrossed and suddenly they were on Andrea's street and Murphy ran ahead to Mrs. Patenaude's door and barked and barked.

"Oh no."

Mrs. P. opened the screen door.

"Murph. Ain't seen you for so long."

She scratched his ears and he stood up with his paws on her shoulders and licked her face. She was one of his favourites and he missed her.

"Candy, nice to see you, honey, c'mon in. Hey, who's your boyfriend? Didn't know you had a boyfriend. Only goes to show. And about time too I'd say. I'm Bernice."

She stuck her hand out and Gerald took it.

"I'm Gerald."

"Oh, I know you, you're the egghead. No use to Andrea. She ain't got two brains to rub together. Just like her father. That's my joke. You're right for Candy here cause she's so smart like a cracker. C'min, c'min, I made cinnamon buns."

They walked in. Gerald was appalled. He'd never seen mess, a total mess, dirt everywhere, just plain dirt. The cinnamon buns were amazing, fat and lashed with sugar and cinnamon.

"Where's Andrea?" asked Candy.

"Working. You know that? At the Red Robin. You were on holidays or you'd know."

"Yeah, we went all the way to the Coast."

"God, I'd love a holiday, but here I am stuck to the old grindstone. I heard from Andrea's father. He's on the oil rigs in Libya, but you gotta hand it to him, sent me a thousand bucks so we can hang onto the old shack. Whataya think of the buns, Gerald?"

"They're very good."

"Oh yes indeed," said Mrs. P., "very good, yaas. Here Murphy, you hound, here's a treat."

He gobbled it up in no time flat. Nobody at home thinks I have a sweet tooth, thought Murphy, but I have.

"Say hello to Andrea when she comes home."

"You know she flunked out, Candy?"

"No."

"Waitress now. No smartern me. Jeez, what a nice dog. Dogs is good, like little kids, they like everybody, ain't figured out yet who they figure is bad. Hey, you bring your little brother over so I can meet him, Norman, yeah, bring him over. Candy, sure nice to see you, you too Gerald, only lighten up a little, a little dirt never killed nobody, I seen your eyes and if I need to I can speak correctly. Bye, Candy, loved seeing you and Murphy and come and see me again."

ANDREA GOT HER JOB AT THE RED ROBIN, AS A waitress, only they called her a service worker. She thought she'd hate working there and she did. She thought if I was lucky I'd of been a robber with Sam. Oh yeah, sure, and end up in jail. So what's this place if it ain't jail? She liked her uniform, a red skirt and blouse with a robin flying over her right breast and a little hat she stuck on the back of her head. She thought she looked sexy. She made a lot of mistakes at first. When everyone came in for lunch she panicked. Old lady Beth they'd all made fun of covered for her and told her how to write things down in order and how to learn the code. Brown cow and fries, chicken over easy and crispy pig. Skinny cow on rye with hot mouseturd. Stuff like that. When kids came in who made fun of her she spit in the soup and smiled nice as apple pie, which they called apple pie, only coffee was called black death with milk, and after work Andrea went to the friendly coffee house down the street and drank her tips and met guys way older than her who read books all the time and she tried two of them and liked one, about a girl who went to the city and met a handsome older man and they were lovers until the wife found out and then she went to London, England to see what the world was like. The other book about boys on an island was stupid. Who cares about boys? A course they'd be stupid. They should put girls on an island, she told the older guys. They said that was a good idea. Andrea sipped her coffee and forgot to show off her breasts. She'd had a good idea. Wow.

"IT'S GOING TO BE TOMORROW, CANDY," SAID Gerald.

"What?"

"The arraignment. You know. Sam and Ramon for robbery."

"Oh."

"I'm going."

Candy said nothing. She sunk into herself. If you breathed small you could sink into yourself.

"I'll tell you about it."

chapter 21

CANDY WOKE UP. SHE OPENED HER EYES AND didn't move a muscle. Sun was out. Curtains were shaking slow, not moving, shaking slow. Ceiling was the same old ceiling, pale blue. Her eyes slipped away, focused again, looked at the wallpaper, and like she was a little kid again she watched the bears and the squirrels and the leaves and the birds and the stream. She'd memorized the pattern but she hadn't looked at it for a long time. She wasn't a little girl anymore. That made her sad. She wiggled her toes. She shut her eyes and thought of her belly. My belly is happy, paid attention to her knees, my knees are okay, looked at her elbow, I got great elbows, looked at her hair but couldn't see out the top of her eyes. She breathed in as far as she could and let the air out slow through her lips which were pushed forward like for a kiss. She decided now it's time to move so she wriggled her toes again.

Boy, are my toes healthy. She could see the sheet move at the bottom of the bed. She saw the blond wood of the headboard. What a nice room. Boy, I'm lucky. She moved her head. Not to look, just to move her head. I'm one of those puzzles you have to find a way to take apart. I wiggled my toes. That was my key. Now I can do anything. I can hear. I can hear Murphy barking. There's a bird. That's a robin. My mom's moving in the kitchen. What's she doing? Dish, dish. Is she baking? In this heat. It must be late. Dad must be gone. Carboy's yelling. Hey, he's yelling, Canny, Canny, where Canny. I'm right here. I'm going to move my fingers. I'll pretend I'm playing a piano. I'm brilliant. I would be if I'd kept up my lessons. I'll start lessons again. I'll tell my mom today I want piano lessons. She'll have a kitten, or an elephant, or a moose, or a beaver. Time to flex my famous muscles. She lifted her legs as high as they'd go. First they had to kick the sheet off. Bicycle, bicycle. They did that in gym. She'd always thought it was dumb. I'll set a new world record. Which was twenty-four. Boring. Arm exercise time. She put her arms out flat, then raised them up and clapped. She did that twice. Boy, is that dumb. Heck, no one can see me so I'll keep doing dumb. Then she did the legs flat and sat up from the hips with her arms behind her head. Then she laughed at herself. Oh, that was out loud. I laughed out loud. She lay back down and didn't move a muscle. She thought. I've never been happier in my whole life. I'm free, I'm free, I'm, I'm okay. I can go to high school. Just like anybody else. I can walk up the cement steps. I can carry books. I can walk into classrooms. I can laugh with girls. I can insult Gerald. Maybe I won't, maybe I won't insult Gerald.

Before she knew it Candy sat up and put her feet on the floor. Then she stood up. I can't take a pee if I don't stand up. I can walk. I can do anything I want. I'm free. She went to the bathroom and then walked downstairs. Her mom was there reading the newspaper.

"Hey, mom, I think I want to take piano lessons."

Her mom stood up, put her hand on Candy's forehead.

"No fever."

"Jeez, mom, can't I want to take piano lessons?"

"Oh yes, Missy, of course, you've been such a pill lately, such a Miss glum, this comes as a great shock. Can I get your cereal?"

"I'll do it, mom."

Her mom thought, I give up. I can't tell what's going on. Raising children is like playing lotto. Once in a while you win. Next she'll want to take Murphy and Norman for a walk.

"Mom can I take Murphy and Carboy for a walk?"

"Yes, you may, indeed yes, yes indeed."

"Okay mom, okay mom."

That girl is making fun of me.

"Hey Carboy, hey Carboy."

He ran in from outside only Candy had to open the door.

"Now be careful with him, Candy, it's a real scorcher today, a real scorcher, Candy."

"Okay, okay, where's his hat at?"

"Perhaps it's near the piano you're going to start playing again."

Murphy was barking.

"Hey Murphy."

Door open.

"That's it, let all the flies and mosquitoes in the house."

"Oh there's one, a skeeter."

Candy swatted her mom's bum. Her mom turned around. She looked at Candy. She was happy. Candy was back to normal, only it wasn't normal. Hitting me on the bum? I'll accept it as a blessing. Now disobey me. Imagine wanting your own daughter to disobey you. I don't care if she does like her father best. I don't care at all, just smile at me again, make fun of me, imagine your own daughter making fun of you and you like it. I can never get her to call him Norman, relax, relax, who cares, who cares, she's normal whatever that is. I know what that is, making meals, doing washing. Awful. I gotta get out of this normal. When Norman's three I'm back to work. The insurance industry has gone straight downhill without me, back in the saddle again, the word processor, I love it, I love it, Candy's happy. Who can tell anything anymore? I'll phone Doug.

chapter 22

CANDY WALKED MURPHY AND CARBOY ACROSS
the street and knocked on Gerald's door. It was
a better door than they had. It was brown wood
with panels. There was a curved window over
the door with coloured glass. Gerald called it a
fanlight. Candy had never been in the house.
Gerald's mother answered. She was always
dressed like she was going out to a party.

"Is Gerald in, please?"

"Oh, you're Candy from across the street.
And this little man is...."

"He's my little brother, Carboy."

"Carboy?"

"Well, he likes playing with cars."

Carboy took two out of his pocket and offered
them to Mrs. Matichek who looked at him.

"This is our dog, Murphy. Sit, Murphy."

He did as he was told and liked the smells of
the house and wanted in to explore.

"I'll get Gerald if you'll just wait a minute."

Candy took Carboy's cars, hid them behind her back and he ran around behind her, then she held them out front. Murphy barked. He liked games, even if he wasn't in them. Carboy squealed, Candy laughed, Murphy barked, Gerald's mom frowned and Gerald grinned and said, "Hi Candy."

"Wanta come for a walk?"

"Sure. See you, mom."

"Yes, Gerald."

She shut the door.

"What's your house like? It looks really cool."

Gerald lifted Carboy in the air and bounced his belly on his head.

"Do again."

He did it again. And again.

"Do you have your own room?"

"One for me, one for my computer."

"Wow."

"It's the right of every kid in our neighbourhood to have a room of our own. Right."

"Sure, dirt bag."

"Candy."

"Mud stuck."

"Candy."

"Yes."

"I thought about Mrs. Patenaude's house and I thought how dirty it was and she knew and I've thought about it. I guess I'm the way I am.

You're so cheerful, I mean except recently, but usually you're optimistic and you like people and I think first of what's wrong with something. Andrea's mom is really –"

"Messy."

"Friendly."

"Murphy likes her house best. Trust a good dog, eh, good dog?"

Murphy stood up on his hind legs and licked Candy's face.

"Oh dog kiss, yuck, thank you, Murph."

They walked in silence to the riverbank where Carboy ran in circles trying to get dizzy and Murphy the dog grinned inside. He'd tried to grin outside but no one noticed.

"Candy? Can I?"

"What?"

"Kiss you."

"Yes."

He did. Just lightly. It wasn't like Ramon. Her knees didn't dissolve. She didn't get shivers. She kissed Gerald back lightly.

"Thank you, Candy. I had a crush on you for three years."

"Holy smoke."

"Dumb, eh?"

Candy grabbed Carboy and swung him around and around like he was an airplane going up and down. Murphy was doing his business and Candy picked it up with a plastic bag and put it in a wooden garbage bin.

"Shit fingers."

"Baby lover."

"Poo brain."

"Bug eyes."

THEY WALKED DOWN TO THE LOWER TRAIL. Candy held Carboy by the hand. If she let go he said, "Canny," and gave back his hand. Murphy ran all over, but if Candy yelled, "Murphy," he came back at once. He wanted to be the best dog on the river walk. Get his ears scratched. He decided the guy was okay. He scratched him now too. He's learning. Candy picked up a stick and threw it and Murphy sped off, spitting gravel.

"When I read about the robbery I thought my life was over. You know about me?"

"I know."

"It was like, I was like terrified. I couldn't get it out of me. I was morose. That's what my mom called me. Sad sack, my dad said, I mean it's lucky I got Carboy to hug. I thought it was all over for me. I'd go to jail."

Murphy had dropped the stick at Candy's feet but she didn't notice. People, thought Murphy, a dog's best friend, some of the time. Carboy had sat down and was playing with an ant. Gerald was looking into Candy's face.

"When you told me yesterday I wasn't named at the arraignment, I felt free."

"They pleaded guilty."

"Tell me again."

"It was short because they both entered guilty pleas. The judge sentenced them right away. They have three years at Kilburn, and can get out in a year and a half. I asked my dad about it. He said the case is closed. The police obviously don't know the identity of the accomplice and if the felons haven't implicated anyone it's over. My dad asked why I was interested. I said I knew them from school and thought I ought to learn how the legal system works. He said, good for me."

"They tricked me. I mean I wouldn't have done it if I'd known but I was dumb."

"And now you're cheerful and optimistic and like people again."

They walked to the next bridge. Carboy was wiped out and Candy rode him on her hip. Then Gerald did. Murphy had gone down to the river to slake his thirst. He was tired. They walked the mile home without a word. Once Gerald put his hand out to help Candy up a hill and then held it.

"Finger cop."

"Weak knees."

"House boy."

"Dog girl."

Murphy barked. C'mon, eh, he barked. Let's go home.

chapter 23

CANDY WOKE NEXT MORNING, AND THE NEXT, and the next, with a black feeling inside her. She'd been having nightmares. They were different each night and yet the same. She was in a city she'd never been in. It was a huge city. She was waiting for a bus that never came. She walked to another stop, and another one. It was always farther away until there were no buildings. She knew she could never catch the bus. Next night she was in a room and stepped through the door into downtown, and with every step she took the streets changed. That happened for a long time. She could never get back to where she started.

She woke up dark inside and scared. She thought each time, I'm okay, I'm okay, it's over, I'm okay, and by breakfast she was Candy again. But every night it was the same. Candy became afraid to go to sleep. She started reading later and later but it didn't matter because she always fell asleep. You couldn't stay awake forever.

School was in two weeks, high school, and most of her class were going to Central. She and Gerald had already agreed to walk together and to study together if anything was tough. Maybe school will make me forget, she thought.

One afternoon she walked to the Red Robin. She'd never gone there since Andrea had become a waitress. She was afraid of what she knew or what she would say. But one day her feet took her there. She didn't plan to go. She felt pulled that way. She walked past the Red Robin, then past it again before she went in. Andrea came over. She looked sexy in her uniform.

"Hey Candyass, haven't seen you forever. Thought you was avoiding me."

"I'll have a Coke, please."

Andrea brought back a Coke and a coffee and sat down and lit a cigarette.

"I'm on my break. You been visitin my mom with that egghead who's in love with you, right, Candy Candy?"

Candy sipped her Coke.

"What's his name? Gerald, yeah. Puppy love. My mother likes your dog."

"I like your mom."

"Livin in my own place now, Candy cane. Hey, I wanna know – know what I wanna know? How come Sam became your friend, cause she was my friend, see, so why you? Cause it made me mad, so why you?"

"I don't know."

"I mean she's tough and you're a wimp."

"I liked her."

"What is it with you, Candy cane, you wanna know tough kids like me, like you were my shadow, and then Sam, so how come?"

"Don't know."

"It's a mystery. And Ramon too, dreamboat Ramon. I don't get it. What they saw in you beats me."

Candy sipped her Coke down to the bottom and made sucking noises with her straw.

"You seen her in jail?"

"No."

"That figures. You just ain't got it, stuck at home all the time with your mom and your dad and your baby and your dog."

"You visited her?"

"Course I do, once a week, bring smokes and chocolate bars. Tell you one thing. You wanna know one thing? We never talk about you. You're nothing, Candy."

Candy left her dollar and walked home. Why would they like me? To use me, sure, to use me. She remembered the kiss. And talking to the man at Radio Shack so Sam could steal a cellphone. I'm so dumb. Why else would I be their friend? I liked it so much, it's true, I did, driving in Ramon's car. To the robbery. Walking over the river with Sam. To the robbery.

ON THE SATURDAY BEFORE SCHOOL CANDY made an appointment to see Sam. She didn't tell her mom and dad. They thought she was at another movie with Gerald. They were in favour of Gerald. He was so polite.

Candy gave her name at the desk at Kilburn, was ushered into a room that had two chairs and a couch and a lamp and pale green walls and an acoustic ceiling and two doors with windows in them. Candy had lots of time to look around before a woman showed Sam in. Sam wore her own clothes. She looked different. She wasn't as big. She looked Candy in the eye and Candy felt like a bug being examined.

"Hi Sam. Here."

Candy gave her a chocolate bar and cookies her mom made. Sam took them.

"How are you?"

"Okay."

Candy didn't know why she was here.

"You lost some weight."

"I work out at the gym."

"How's Ramon?"

"Your dreamboat. Don't see him. Guys are in another part of the place. Still looks good, little Candy."

"How's Rhonda?"

"Dunno. She's crazy, hits everyone, stuck in solitary, gets out and goes for an attendant, back in, went for me, I decked her, she's gone, ain't got a chance, don't care what she does."

"She scared me."

"Did I?"

"No."

"Shoulda been scared, Miss Virgin, shoulda been."

"I have nightmares about being caught. Why did you do it? Why didn't you tell?"

That's why I'm here, thought Candy, to know why I'm free.

"Are you crazy? Tell the cops something? Tell em nothing, nothing at all. You don't know anything, do you, green as grass. Got to be that monkey, see no, hear no, tell no."

"What will you do when you get out?"

"I ain't gonna get caught, that's for sure, leave this crummy town, I'll be okay."

"I'm sorry you were caught."

"Not half as sorry as me, honey, but jail's a lot bettern school."

"It can't be."

"You go to your school. I'll go to mine. There's the buzzer, time's up, on your way home, Candy."

Candy stood up to go. Sam put out her hand and Candy shook it, then stood on her tiptoes and quickly kissed her on the cheek, turned and left, and decided to walk the two miles home, all mixed up about Sam who used her, protected her, was mean to her, was nice to her. Doesn't matter, thought Candy, I'll just like her anyway.

SAM WENT BACK TO HER ROOM FROWNING. SHE ate a cookie. She didn't like to be unsure, but she was unsure about Candy, one of the pretty girls, one of the school girls. Candy was kinda dumb. But she likes me, thought Sam, she does. I should like her. She kissed me. She didn't have to. I'll ease off. I'll hate good girls except Candy. Wouldn't put her in a scam again. I'll protect her. If she needed it. I'd protect her. Yeah.

WHEN CANDY WAS HALFWAY HOME SHE SAW the guy again who took stuff out of garbage cans. He was old and bald and smelled. She stopped. He looked at her, right through her and bent into the next garbage can. He wore old jeans and running shoes and a torn plaid shirt and had his old bike. He didn't seem to care if anyone watched. He pulled three pop cans out of the garbage and dropped them in one of his plastic bags. When she'd seen him before Candy had always gone the other way. He was scary. He was really dirty.

"Sir, can I help? I've got seven dollars if you want?"

He looked at her then, hard. He had big, grey eyebrows. He held out his hand. She gave him the money. He took it in his fist.

"Bye sir."

Candy walked away and wondered, what if I was like that? Did he have a mom and dad? Will Sam be like that if she keeps being a crook? She's tough. That guy's tough too. He's still alive. Or he's dumb. Was he in school? Rhonda's a loser. Why does she hate? Look at the geraniums in that window box. They're beautiful. Everything is so green, just fat with green. The lawns are fire green. They're burning green in the sun. Rhonda would hit me for sure. I don't know how to hit. I can't even hit a baseball. These yards are so neat. Not like Sam's apartment. Boy, was that a mess. Living off an alley. That was great. I wonder who Ramon is, I mean really. Gerald has the low-down on teachers at Central. Get Ms. Mac-Intosh for English, if you're lucky. I'm lucky. Will I keep going to movies with Gerald? Should I let him kiss me each time? Yes and yes. That's settled. It's not like Ramon. Ramon the betrayer. I'll write a comic book and put him in it. Why'd I kiss Sam? I dunno. I can't know everything. I'll take Carboy for a walk when I get home. What movie did I see? What'll I tell mom? I'm in a quandary. Spell quandary. There's

Andrea's house. Ain't been painted since the Flood. Grass ain't been mowed for a decade. I gave that old guy my seven bucks. I guess I'm a nice person. Don't brag, Candy. Why'd I do it? I dunno. I can't know everything. It's an enigma. Spell enigma. I'm ready for high school with words like quandary and enigma and delectable and sequential, dope bucket, heifer head, I'm ready for high school, no doubt about it.

When Candy woke up next morning something was different. She did the toe wiggle, the hand clap, the sit-up, the lay down, counted the squirrels, oh my gosh, school! leapt up, washed, dressed, ran downstairs.

"About time," said her mom, "about time, missy."

That's one.

"Your hair's a bird nest. For heaven's sake, Candy, comb it, for heaven's sake."

That's two. She combed her hair.

"Don't pick at your cereal, eat it."

That's three. Candy ate the cereal. It was hard to because she was nervous. High school, high school. It was so big. Stopped mid-spoon. She forgot what she was doing.

"Candy? You okay? You had your dad and I worried sick. What was wrong?"

"Nothin."

"Must have been something. You weren't yourself. Candy."

"Gotta go, mom."

Hug, hug, and she was gone out the door and over to Gerald's.

"Hey, egghead," she said.

"Banana brain."

"Noname nerd."

"Hot lips."

"I'm nervous, are you?"

"No way," said Gerald.

"Are so."

"It's just school. It's with you I'm nervous."

"Excellent."

They walked to the end of the block. Suddenly Candy realized she didn't have a nightmare last night. Wow. She did a quick hopscotch.

"Candy!"

"What."

"You're not a little girl anymore."

No I'm not, thought Candy. I know Andrea, Sam, Ramon, I've been in a robbery, been guilty, been scared, and now I'm free. Freedom. I can do what I want. So to heck with Sam and I'll see you when you get out and I'll go to the Red Robin after school. She did a quick hopscotch again.

"Baby girl."

"Head bone."

Candy grimaced to Gerald who shook his head. She did another jump.

"Good grief. You're in high school now."

That's one.

about the author

DON KERR IS THE AUTHOR OF FIVE BOOKS of poetry, seven plays, a short fiction collection and a non-fiction book on the history of the city of Saskatoon. *Candy on the Edge* is his first work of teen fiction.

He has edited three play anthologies, several poetry anthologies, and Coteau's comprehensive book of Anne Szumigalski's poetry, *On Glassy Wings*. He has also served as an editor with the periodicals *Next Year Country*, *GRAIN* and *NeWest Review*.

Don Kerr was born in Saskatoon, where he still lives and works.